M000311907

Fate Ball

A Novel

Fate Ball

A Novel

Adam W. Jones

Fate Ball

This is a work of fiction. All of the characters, organizations, and events portrayed in this novel are either products of the author's imagination or are used fictitiously.

Cover and Interior design by Ted Ruybal

Manufactured in the United States of America

Wisdom House Books

For more information, please contact:

www.wisdomhousebooks.com

www.adamwjones.com

Hardback ISBN: 978-0-692-57830-8

Paperback ISBN: 978-0-692-47534-8

Ebook ISBN: 978-0-9972118-0-1

LCCN: 2015957933

FIC000000—FICTION / General

FIC043000—FICTION / Coming of Age

1 2 3 4 5 6 7 8 9 10

To my wife Susan and
daughters Lilly and Ainslie
for showing me the meaning
of true love.

Acknowledgements

Writing can be easy, but finishing a book is very difficult. I want to thank my wife, Susan, for believing in me and motivating me to finish *Fate Ball.* To my parents, Susie and Dave Jones, who have always been supportive of whatever I have done, whether they agreed with my decision or not. To my first editor, Cathy East, who inspired me to write this book in the first place and who believed in my "voice." To my editor, Arielle Hebert, who gave me wonderful suggestions to make this story more complete. To Ted Ruybal and Wisdom House Books for their patience with a new author and their professional process from start to finish. And to Ava for planting the seed.

Prologue

Palmetto Memorial Gardens
Charleston, South Carolina

—February 1994—

It was the perfect day for a funeral.

A light drizzle fell from gray skies that hung like a wet blanket over the mourners. Umbrellas sprouted like mushrooms around a main tent where the family sat in two neat rows of eight chairs each. Friends and strangers huddled together offering moral support and protection from the late February chill. A few hardy souls withstood the rain and bone-jarring wind in knee-length raincoats with collars flipped up for maximum protection.

It certainly was not your typical Charleston weather, but everyone seemed to manage.

Able Curran stood under an ancient sea oak tree about seventy-five yards away from the mourners. He had arrived a good hour before the others and watched in solitude as a convoy of limousines, Suburbans, and Towncars pulled up and mourners poured out. At first he was surprised by the number of people in attendance, easily three hundred, but then he understood when he thought of how many lives she had touched—or ruined—depending on how you looked at it.

I wonder how many people will come to my funeral, he thought.

He had not seen her in ten years. Ten long years . . . nearly four thousand days. And rarely had he lived through a single one without thinking about her at least once . . . if not twice.

Whoever said, "First loves never die," was right, and most likely speaking from experience.

A week earlier, Able received the call from her sister. He knew that any call from her family would not be good news. It never was.

"Hello, Able, it's Lovey."

Able took a breath and braced for the bad news. "Is she going to be okay?"

"She's gone."

The call lasted only a few minutes. Just long enough for Able to find out the funeral arrangements and pass along his condolences to the family. Everyone knew this time would come, but it was still a shock when it had finally happened.

Ava Dubose had a feline prowess when it came to averting death that confounded many of her doctors over the years. There were at least two incidents of overdosing and one beating she took from a dealer that put her in the hospital for weeks. The family stopped counting the near-misses and just clung to the hope that she would not be found dead in a ditch somewhere.

In the end, a syringe of bad heroine was all it took to take her life. And turn Able's life upside-down.

Able hung up the phone and slumped back in his large leather "Daddy" chair. He stared into space and rubbed his temples to try and ease his mind, but it was hopeless. His eyes filled quickly, and the tears gushed, like a broken dam. Not the first he'd shed for her, and probably not the last. The sudden surge of emotion lasted only a few minutes, but it drained him completely. *Deep breath*, he said to himself. *Deep breath*.

Able heard the front door slam open, and laughter flowed toward him like a sudden breeze.

"Daddy, Daddy, Daddy, guess what?" shouted his six-year-old daughter, Maggie.

Able quickly wiped his eyes with both hands and sat up tall in the chair.

Maggie rounded the corner and leaped into his arms.

"How's my baby girl?"

"Great, Daddy, look, I got a gold star on my math quiz!"

"That's fabulous, honey bun. I'm so proud of you."

But Able should have known he couldn't hide anything from Maggie. She stared at him hard, then grabbed his face and held it in her little doll-like hands.

"Why were you crying, Daddy? Are you okay?"

"Yes, sweetie, Daddy is fine. I just got some sad news. That's all."

"Don't be sad, Daddy." She leaned into him and hugged his neck tightly for a moment. Then she pushed back quickly. "Hey, I know what will cheer you up. I'll get you a glass of milk and some Oreos. Will that make you feel better, Daddy?"

"That would be great, sweetie. Thank you so much."

Maggie jumped from her father's lap and ran toward the kitchen. She stopped at the doorway and turned back with a grin on her face.

"And a few Oreos for me, too, Daddy?"

"Of course, sweetie. I can't eat alone now, can I?"

Maggie smiled wide, scooted around her mother who was in the doorway, then ran to the pantry in the kitchen.

Able turned up his collar against the wind and blinked hard. Remembering Maggie and the Oreos made him laugh and cry at the same time. He folded his arms and squeezed himself tighter to stave off the cold. The rain soaked his hair and chilled him to the bone. Even the broad cover of the old tree could not keep all the rain off on this dreadful day.

The congregation began to say the Lord's Prayer, and Able heard the familiar words as they drifted across the cemetery. He joined in and spoke softly, just for himself. But he choked on "and lead us not into temptation, but deliver us from evil." The monotone words from the others lingered in the air like a swirl of smoke from a grandfather's pipe.

Temptation is what changed his life . . . for better and for worse.

Ava called it "Fate Ball."

Chapter One

Savannah, Georgia

—September 1980—

Ava Dubose lay in her queen-size bed surrounded by throw pillows in various shades of orange and red. Some had tassels, others were made of shiny fabrics, but they all went well with the multicolored duvet cover that draped over the foot of her four-poster bed. She wore a pink sleeping mask, with "Princess" embroidered across the front, to keep out the morning light, but she was unable to sleep any more this morning. She stretched her arms in the air and pointed her toes toward the footboard in her early morning, full-body stretch.

She swung her legs around and sat on the edge of the bed in her nightgown—a red-and-white tie-dyed R.E.M. T-shirt that was two sizes too big. She pulled off the mask and threw it on her bedside table, where it settled on top of her new *Cosmo* with the headline "New Ways to Make Your Man Melt." She leaned her head to one side and then to the other until there was a pop in her neck. Then she rotated her head atop her long, luxurious neck to work out the other kinks.

Ava stood up slowly and shuffled across the room to the chest of drawers that stood in the corner of her small, private dorm room. It was an old piece of furniture that had been passed down from mother to daughter. Her grandmother used it when she attended St. Margaret's, then Ava's mother, and now it was Ava's turn. If she didn't destroy it in the next few years, maybe her daughter, God willing, would carry on the tradition.

St. Margaret's really hadn't changed much since it was founded in the early 1900s. It was a two-year women's college that had a conservative curriculum for conservative girls from conservative families. The only reason St. Margaret's accepted Ava was because she was a third-generation legacy. The administration had been regretting that decision ever since.

The dresser's antique white paint was cracked in places and a few of the original brass pulls were missing, but it was a fine piece of furniture just the same. The ornate carvings on the front of the drawers, the spindle legs with wooden wheels, and the delicate scroll that ran just above the top of the chest to a peak at the center showed the quality craftsmanship in the hundred-year-old piece.

A small lamp on top of the chest illuminated several photographs in neat, silver frames. The first photo was of Ava with her little sister when she was five and Lovey was one. Ava was holding her in her arms and smiling wide, the proud big sister. The second was of her mother and father during their salad days—about ten years ago. She hadn't seen them smile like that since she was a little girl. The last photograph was of Ava sitting in her grandmother's lap as they rocked away an afternoon at the family beach cottage. She loved "Grande" more than anything.

Ava picked up the photograph of her grandmother and kissed it sweetly. Then she placed it face down on the chest.

She pulled open the second drawer from the top, her underwear drawer, and slid her hand under the pile of clean panties. She pulled out a fifth of Absolut vodka and unscrewed the cap. Ava put the bottle to her lips and leaned her head back slowly. The vodka *glug, glugged* out of the bottle and down her throat. She closed her eyes for a moment to allow the alcohol to warm her body. She took one more good swig, then screwed the cap back on tightly. She slid the bottle to the back of her underwear drawer and covered it with cotton, silk, and lace. Finally she pulled out a fresh pair of basic white cotton underpants that she would wear that day and tossed them on the bed. Ava picked up the photograph of her grandmother, kissed it again, and put it back in its rightful place.

This was her morning ritual.

Chapter Two

There was no way to know that by the end of the night Able Curran would experience the perfect young man's fantasy.

But it happened just the same.

Able was a nice, quiet boy who kept to himself. He didn't drink much, except for sneaking a beer once in a while when his parents were away. He dated even less since he concentrated more on playing guitar and surfing, which left little time to chase girls.

Able moved back into his parent's house after returning from a year-long sojourn across Europe a few months ago. He really wasn't ready for college, so he spent his junior and senior years working odd jobs to save up for the journey. His stepfather refused to pay for anything other than college, much less a headman trip across Europe. His real dad was too busy chasing co-eds to care about what Able wanted to do.

"I'm not going to bankroll you traipsing around Europe, drinking and smoking weed," said his stepfather sternly. "My father made me go straight to college, so that's what you need to do. If not, then you're on your own, pal."

Able stood up to his stepfather and said he didn't need his stinking charity. Able never got over the fact that this prick was sleeping with his mother and he hated being called "pal." His stepfather was surprised a month after high school graduation when Able flashed his airline tickets and six-month Eurail Pass.

"I've got an extra $8,000 in traveler's checks too," Able said with attitude. "Stick that in your pipe and smoke it, pal."

After he returned home nearly penniless, he had to crawl back to his parents' place to crash for a while. Able was anxious to move along with his life.

Pete Fenster, a friend from high school who was attending the local Savannah College, had invited Able to their Saturday night party at the fraternity house. All of his friends called him Fen. Good looking, great athlete, good grades without trying, he was the All-American kid in the group who did everything well. Girls adored him. He was the envy of many, but Able was not the competitive type and just enjoyed having a good friend.

But when Saturday night came, Fen had to practically drag Able out of his childhood bedroom kicking and screaming to the party.

"Let go, Fen," Able said, pulling away. "You know I'm not a party guy. I think I'll just stay here and work on this Clapton tune. It's got bar chords that I need to work on."

"Yeah, right," said Fen. "You'll just sit up in your room whacking off to your *Playboy* collection all night, you disgusting little creep."

Able winced at how close Fen came to the truth.

Able's room had not changed in any significant way since he was twelve. The model airplanes still dangled from the ceiling, taking flight when the ceiling fan was on. His Little League baseball "participant" trophies (there were three) shared the bookshelf with his G.I. Joe, Dr. Seuss books, and his sizable penny collection.

Able had sort of been in a holding pattern since then. The doctors (all four of them) said basically the same thing: that it was a product of his parents' separation and ultimate divorce.

"Come on, Able," Fen insisted, "Come meet some *real* girls for a change. All you do is work at the store, practice guitar all night long, and daydream about things that will never come true. There's a frat house full of lovelies down the street just waiting to get plucked. So let's go live a little, man!"

"Don't you think it's kind of late?" Able stalled. He looked at his watch. "It's already after ten—"

"What are you, fifty?" Fen cried. "Come on, man! The party's just getting started!"

"I don't know . . ."

"I'm not taking no for an answer!" Fen insisted. "Somebody's gotta save you from yourself—and I need a wingman! Now get your ass in gear!"

"All right, all right!" Able sighed. He knew Fen—once he got an idea in his head, nothing could sway him. He figured he might as well give in to the inevitable. "Just let me grab my glasses."

He and Fen walked the six blocks from the Curran home down to the Kappa Phi house on the edge of campus. Even before they reached the fraternity house, they could hear music bellowing from the speakers and "yahoos!" coming from the partygoers who sounded well into their cups. The Kappa Phi house was a beautiful Tudor-style stone mansion on the outside, but the inside was now mired in frat-boy filth.

Able was given a beer within ten seconds of walking through the door.

A minute later someone gave him a shot of Tequila. No salt. No lime.

By the time Able made his way from the front of the house to the back patio, he was feeling just fine.

A full pig turned slowly on a spit in the backyard . . . pulled pork BBQ North Carolina style cooked over hardwood coals with real coleslaw and crisp hushpuppies. The sweet smell of hickory wafted through the backyard as plumes of white smoke billowed from the well-worn cooker. Kegs chilled in ice-filled rubber trash barrels that lined the edge of the back patio, so you were never far from a refill. A rickety card table at the end of the buffet held at least thirty bottles of every brand of liquor you could name. Music from a frat band shook the house and pulsed out through the sliding-glass door toward the back patio. The yard was mobbed with kids—laughing, flirting, dancing and stumbling about.

It was one of those sweltering hot days of early September in the South, the kind that made you sweat the moment you step outside. The party had started in the heat of the afternoon football game, and now, at eleven o'clock at night, it was still ninety degrees, for God's sake. The frat boys wore standard-issue khakis and blue blazers with a white or blue button-down. The girls wooed the boys with their colorful short skirts or summer dresses—some with spaghetti straps, some with loop straps, and some that seemed held up by pure magic.

As usual, Fen launched himself into the crowd while Able stood along the edges, wondering how to wade in. But the scenery was good, and the booze was free-flowing. And

soon Able was surprised at how much he was enjoying himself. He danced for an hour straight—by himself, mind you, but girls were in close proximity.

But after doing three rapid-fire Tequila shots, and shaking it up to Squeeze's "Take Me I'm Yours," Able threw up on a bush at the edge of the dance floor. He wiped his mouth, looked around for witnesses, then stumbled inside to find a place to lie down.

Just as he was about to tumble over an ottoman in the Reading Room, Fen appeared out of nowhere and dragged him upstairs to a distant bathroom. Fen held him up by the arm to keep Able from falling face-first onto the tile floor. He leaned Able against the sink and splashed water on his face, then made him swill some mouthwash before just as swiftly dragging him back down to the party.

"Come on, Able, pull yourself together, man. How are you going to pick up a girl if you can't even stand up? Here, drink some water for a while, or you'll never last." He picked up a random cup of beer, dumped it out, and scooped up some slushy ice and water from around one of the kegs. Then he left Able with his cup of water on the couch in the foyer and went back to his nightly quest.

Able woke up from a short drunken nap when he felt ice water sloshing down his leg and tried to focus. He saw Fen through the archway to the library hitting on a cute freshman from Wilson, North Carolina. Fen had found her photo in the freshman directory and picked her out as his early-semester goal. She leaned back against the bookshelf that lined the room looking like the ubiquitous excited freshman—a constant smile with just a hint of a deer-in-the-headlights look in her eyes. She was wearing Fen's blazer—he'd offered it to her when the temperature dropped a few degrees, and she just couldn't refuse such a gentlemanly gesture, even in this heat. The blazer hung just below her short pink skirt, so all you could see were her thin, tan legs and avocado green espadrilles. Her enormous brown eyes sparkled as she looked up in full-flirt mode. She giggled and tossed her sun-streaked brown hair with a flick of her head at the slightest hint of humor. Fen took a sip of his drink, then rested his hand on the bookshelf beside her head, leaning in close to whisper something in her ear. She giggled again, slapped at him playfully, then flicked her hair.

Able shook his head. *How did guys figure out how to do this stuff?*

Suddenly the front door swung open with a bang, and he strained to see what was going on.

One by one he watched them catwalk through the front door like models on a runway—the next more beautiful than the one before. It was a full-on assault of bleached-blonde hair, sparkling white teeth, and pure youthful exuberance. Able had never seen that many beautiful girls in

one place before, except maybe in one of the *Playboys* that he hid beneath his mattress at home. The right side of his mattress was a good three inches higher than the other, but no one had discovered his stash yet . . . or admitted to it anyway.

The girls bounded into the room with their blonde hair bouncing and glistening in the light of the chandelier that hung from the vaulted ceiling at the center of the foyer, the only remaining evidence of a once-grand fraternity house. The boys nearby stood drooling like a bunch of dopes looking at the Blonde-Squad beauties. Some of the girls were drooling, too, but most likely out of envy.

And then he saw her.

She was the fifth and last girl through the doorway. She had a presence that commanded attention. Just seeing her gave Able a shot of adrenaline that sobered him up for the moment. The music and talking stopped, and just like in the movies, the girl seemed to move in slow motion. Every sound that entered his head went silent and everything around him outside of her form faded to a blur.

He was mesmerized by her exquisite beauty. She had platinum blonde hair pulled back from her forehead in a poufy fifties style and held in place by a tortoise-shell headband. She had flawless skin—smooth, lightly tanned—and striking blue eyes. Her face was the best of Raquel Welch and Christy Brinkley combined. All atop a curvaceous body that would make Rubens drop his paintbrush. She was the most beautiful girl he had ever seen in his life—and that included Miss August 1980.

She exuded a confidence and sex appeal not found in many young girls experiencing the unfettered freedom of college life for the first time. Most of the other girls wore the standard issue designer outfits in shades of pink and green. Nice, mind you, but conservative and mother approved. This girl wore tall cowboy boots that came up to her knees, then a little skin, then a short, pleated black skirt that hugged her at the belly button, then a white button-down shirt tied in a knot at her waist. She wore classic single pearl earrings with a matching pearl necklace, but her wrists were swallowed up in a tangle of bracelets in silver, gold, and a variety of beads, large and small. None of it mother approved, except for maybe the pearls.

Her head pivoted gracefully on her long, thin neck as she turned and caught Able in full gawk. A Cheshire-cat grin curled across her perfect pink lips and revealed a smile that knocked the wind out of him like a punch in the stomach.

She had found her prey.

Able would never understand why he was chosen. It may have been because he didn't look like a typical fresh-faced frat boy in khakis, a button-down, and hair nicely cropped and parted to one side. Okay, so he was wearing a white button-down shirt, but the rest was totally nonstandard frat boy issue—torn jeans and brown suede boots and long brown hair. It could have been all those things that made her choose him, or was he just the most easily accessible, semiconscious male in the room?

Whatever the reason, all the manners his mother beat into him as a kid must have sunk in deep, because he instinctively stood up to greet her as she approached. He smiled politely and nodded hello, but she pushed him back on the couch with a light shove that would have toppled any drunk. And, boy, was Able drunk. She stood over him as he slumped and settled on the couch with his legs outstretched in a textbook drunken sprawl. He looked up at her in awe as she leaned forward and placed a hand on his shoulder. Then she climbed on the couch one leg at a time and straddled his lap. Able couldn't understand why this beautiful girl was sitting on top of him, but he wasn't about to ask questions. Sometimes you just have to take what comes your way, and he was happy just to let the moment happen.

She sat on top of him and caressed his cheek with the back of her hand. "You're adorable," she said as she looked deep into his eyes. She held his face in her hands, then leaned in close and kissed him.

It was the kind of kiss that makes you melt into the other person so completely you need a moment to gather your thoughts when you come up for air. At first it was a very polite lip-to-lip kiss, the way you might kiss your cousin or something—your cute girl cousin. Then their lips parted and the heat from her mouth rushed into his, and the kiss quickly became much more than the kissing-cousins variety. It was soft and sensual, not the kind of spit-swap one would expect at a drunken frat party. The next thing Able knew, she softly bit his bottom lip, then sucked on it for a second before kissing him again the regular French way. The bite didn't bother him much. He was never into that kind of thing, but now he found he really liked it. The minute-long kiss was perfect and unlike any Able had ever experienced. It didn't seem like their first kiss, but like they had kissed a million times before.

She pulled away slowly as Able looked up at her longingly, wanting more.

She smiled, climbed off his lap, and stood over him. Able knew he must look like a complete dope sitting there in post-kiss pucker, all slack-jawed and goo-goo-eyed, but he didn't care. She leaned in to straighten his glasses that were knocked askew, then offered her hand and helped him up from the couch. He stumbled slightly, since the floor was slippery with beer. He looked into her eyes, and she looked back at him with a perfect look on her face. Her blue eyes smoldered and her mouth curled in a half grin.

Able had the feeling that this girl could make him happy, and he hoped it would be longer than just this one night would allow.

“I’m late for curfew,” she said in a sexy Southern accent. “So I’ve really gotta go, but you have to call me. Okay?”

Outside of a French accent and maybe Italian, Able thought the sexiest accent had to be a soft, sophisticated Southern belle accent. Of course, it helped when the person with the accent was beautiful. Even the sexiest accent wouldn’t help a three-hundred-pound trailer bride, unless she worked for one of those phone sex lines and you never actually laid eyes on her.

Able tried to answer her, but what came out of his mouth certainly wasn’t English. In a matter of minutes, being in her presence turned him into a real mess. His head was thinking of all these great things to say, but his mouth refused to work at all. This must be what his father meant when he said that women were all-powerful and could make the biggest, strongest man fall to his knees and cry like a baby. Able wasn’t about to cry, but he sure sounded like a baby just standing there gurgling and cooing.

"Do you have a pen, darlin'?" she asked in her sweet accent. "I'll give you my number, so we can maybe go out sometime." He stood there like a complete dope, still unable to form words, and just shook his head "no."

"You stay right here and don't move a muscle," she said sternly, grabbing his shoulders to reinforce the command. Then she disappeared into the crowd and left him standing there in a perfect-kiss-induced stupor.

His head was racing as he tried to comprehend what just happened. Was he that drunk? Maybe he was having a simple daydream, or a full-on dream and he was fast asleep in his cozy bed waiting for the real fireworks to begin? *Cool*, he thought, *a porn dream*. The blonde seductress and the others in the Blonde Squad must be changing into skimpy lingerie right now about to engulf him in a tidal wave of hot blondness. He thought of all the naughty possibilities and drew on his limited porn-viewing past and the "Playboy Advisor" submissions for ideas. Unfortunately, he could only come up with a few R-rated scenarios.

The blonde seductress returned a moment later holding a red Magic Marker. Able continued to stand there with his feet firmly planted on the beer-soaked floor, still not able to utter a single word. She looked into his eyes and smiled as she placed the Magic Marker between her teeth and took hold of his new button-down shirt. With

a quick tug, she sent buttons flying across the room like miniature skeet. Able stood there dumbfounded with his shirt pulled open and just laughed at the craziness of the moment. He glanced around to see if anyone was watching, but everyone seemed to be in their own little worlds. Couples huddled in the dark corners making out. Girls and guys continued to flirt with the hopes of making out before they passed out. No one even noticed what was going on ten feet away and no one cared that Able was in the middle of his very own fantasy. This made him question the reality of the moment, but he wasn't about to wake up now.

With great flair, the girl uncapped the pen with her teeth and spat the top across the room. His eyes followed the cap as it bounced into the corner and spun several times before coming to a stop. But then his eyes were riveted on her as she got down on her knees and looked up at him with a she-devil look in her eyes.

She grabbed his belt buckle and pulled him close, then took the pen and began writing across his unimpressive torso, laughing and smiling with each stroke. She started out low, just above his belly button and worked her way up to his hairless chest. He stood there motionless. Even in his drunken stupor Able sucked in his gut and puffed out his chest. Guys want to look good just like girls do—even when they're shit-faced. He gave her his best hard body look, even though it was still a bit soft around the edges. He squirmed a little bit when the Magic Marker moved across sensitive areas, since he was kind of tick-lish. When she noticed a flinch, or giggle, she made that line extra bold just to watch him squirm.

"There!" she said when finished. "Now you have no excuse for not calling me ah um . . ."

"Able. Name's Able," he slurred.

Able looked down at his chest and stomach to try and decipher her number, but he couldn't see anything very clearly. The lighting wasn't the greatest in the foyer, plus he'd smudged his glasses pretty badly when they were kissing. She grabbed his belt buckle again and pulled him in for another kiss. They wrapped their arms around each other and kissed like he'd just returned from six months of active duty. It was like the old photograph on the cover of *LIFE* magazine after World War II when that sailor grabbed a girl out of the crowd and laid a big ol' kiss on her in right there in the middle of the street. Just like that sailor, Able was feeling pure joy, for sure.

She leaned in close, gently held the back of his head in her hand, and whispered in his ear, "Call me tomorrow, darlin'." She kissed him on the cheek, then turned quickly and disappeared through the front door.

Able staggered after her as far as the front stoop and watched her skip down the walkway toward her friends, who waited in the parking lot. They all piled into an old powder blue Jeep Wagoneer with fake wood side panels and just enough rust to hold the old tin can together. Laughter and high-pitched squeals flowed from the windows as the car full of girls sped past the fraternity house on the way to hopefully making curfew.

Able stumbled to the street and watched the Wagoneer's taillights flash red at the stop sign at the end of the road. Then, with a blinker-less left turn and a screech of tires against the pavement, the car—and the girl—disappeared into the night.

Chapter Three

The morning sun beat through Able's shadeless windows and turned his bedroom into an oven. The combination of heat and hangover made it impossible to sleep late. He woke up with a pounding headache and a mouthful of cotton. He had been too drunk the night before to remember the "two aspirin and a glass of water before bed" rule.

Groaning, Able sat on the edge of his bed, rubbed his tired eyes, smacked his dry lips, and swore to never drink that much again.

He dragged his stiff body out of bed and into the bathroom to somehow try to revive himself. He leaned in about two inches from the mirror and saw a pitiful sight.

A nineteen-year-old boy after five hours of sleep and a raging hangover wasn't pretty.

He splashed cold water on his face, toweled off, and cleaned the smudges off his glasses before putting them

on to see his world in focus. He was still wearing the shirt from last night and noticed that it was torn. Most of the buttons were missing. The memories of the previous night seeped through the haze of a massive hangover.

"What the hell—?" he said out loud, tugging at his shirt. He could see red marks on his chest and stomach. "Hoolllyyy shit—it wasn't a dream!"

He quickly pulled off his shirt and stood in front of the full-length mirror attached to the back of his bathroom door. He bent and twisted his body to try and decipher the phone number the beautiful girl had written across his torso. After several minutes of yoga-like moves, he was pretty sure that he had broken the code. It had to be her real number, he thought. Who would go to such great lengths and then write a fake phone number across a guy's body?

"Yoo-hoo, honey, you up?" his mother called out. She knocked on his bedroom door and peeked in. "Breakfast is ready."

"I'm up, I'm up!" Able shouted as he grabbed a robe for cover. The last thing he needed was for his mother to see a girl's phone number emblazoned across his chest in red marker. He didn't think she would understand, and even if she did, he was not in the mood to get the "nice-girls-don't-do-that-type-of-thing" speech.

Able heard stories of how his parents had been the perfect academic couple at Savannah College . . . she an Art History professor and he a professor of Advanced English Literature. They were both relatively young newlyweds and both attractive, and the combination had made it easier to get caught up in the fad of swapping partners at parties. They both had enjoyed the swinging seventies way too much, and once it ended they couldn't recover from the damage done by their dual infidelity. His mother remarried quickly (to one of her key partners), a Biology professor, and Able tolerated his new stepfather. At age thirteen Able took up guitar and spent most of the next five years in his bedroom practicing and listening to music. His mother and his stepfather didn't seem to have much time for him and let him come and go as he pleased. Since all of his parents were professors at Savannah College, it made for some awkward times around town when they bumped into one another.

Able was consistently embarrassed by his father who easily transitioned back into the single lifestyle and was not opposed to a short-term fling with other professors, associates, or even students. He never dated anyone for more than a semester. He earned a reputation for saving young female students, who might be struggling in his class, with a letter grade increase for each base rounded. If you were flunking, then a home run was needed to get an A, and many girls over the years rounded the bases just to ensure a high GPA.

Able was still not ready for the stresses of college, and his mother insisted that he live at home, work, and save money. It seemed like a pretty good idea at first—free

meals, a free housekeeper, and most important, free rent.

He soon realized that there was a huge downside to living at home—and not being able to bring girls back to his bachelor pad was number one on the list. Not to say it would have happened, mind you, but at least there would have been the possibility of romance once in a while. He could have dealt with dirty clothes, a messy apartment, PB&Js and mac & cheese as the staples of his diet, and scrimping by each month on his paltry earnings. It would have been worth it, though, to be able to say to a willing young co-ed, "Let's go back to my place for a beer or something." Able made it through breakfast with his robe cinched tightly. His mother didn't have a clue about the hidden number and Able wanted to keep it that way.

Able paced back and forth in his room practicing his lines until lunchtime to make the call. For one thing, he didn't want to appear too eager, although given what he looked like and what she looked like, it was pretty easy to determine who would be the one to pine away. Plus, he needed several hours to put together a game plan so he wouldn't sound like a complete idiot.

She answered on the third ring.

"Hello," she said in that sweet Southern accent.

Just hearing her voice again sent tingles down his spine and caused his game plan to instantly evaporate from his brain. *What a dope*, he thought.

"Heeyy, heellloo there," he said, sounding like an idiot. "I don't, uh, know if you remember me or not," he stammered. "But, uh, we, uh, kinda met last night at the fraternity house . . ."

"Is this the adorable boy I pounced on last night?" she said with a light-hearted laugh.

"Uhh, yep, that's me, the pouncee," Able said, trying to play the humor card. *Damn*, he said to himself, *don't start rhyming, you idiot!*

She laughed kindly at his attempt at humor, then cleared her throat. "Look," she said in a more serious tone. "I'm really not that kind of girl. This morning a friend told me what I did, and I'm just so embarrassed. I guess I had one too many shots of Jagermeister last night and got carried away."

Able made a mental note to buy a bottle of Jagermeister as soon as he hung up the phone.

"Hey, that's okay," he said, trying to sound like it didn't matter. He fumbled over his words and tried to prepare himself for her to end their relationship before it ever got started. All Able could do now was appear like he was just going along for the ride—no emotion and no disappointment after their fifteen-minute tryst.

"I was wasted too . . . really wasted . . . man, was I wasted. Not a big deal, though, really . . . it's not . . . ahh . . . a big

deal." He laughed a pathetic laugh.

But it was a big deal . . . his heart sank. He didn't know what to say. She was so out of his league, he should have known better than to get his hopes up. He quickly convinced himself that she and her girlfriends all planned to find patsies last night, mess with their heads, and then cut them loose the next day. They were probably all having a good laugh right now—a big ol' beautiful-blonde-girls-whipping-their-hair-around-in-the-dorm-room laugh. There was probably a prize for the most emotional damage done, like bubble bath or perfume.

There was a long, awkward silence, and Able almost hung up out of shear embarrassment.

"You know," she said softly, "I don't even know your full name."

"It's Able," he said, wincing as his voice cracked. "I mean . . . I'm Able Curran."

"Ummm . . ." She made a sound like she had just taken a bite of her favorite mint chocolate chip ice cream. "I've always *loved* the name Able. He was the good son, right?"

"Uh, yes he was . . . but I don't have to be."

"My name is Ava, A-V-A. Ava Dubose."

"Ava, A-V-A," he said, spelling it out. "An interesting name for an interesting girl."

Ava laughed, hopefully at the situation and not at Able. She had one of those incredibly sexy laughs that couldn't be learned—it was purely God given. You know, kind of a soft and lilting laugh with a geisha-girl finish.

"Yeah, well," she said a bit sheepishly. "My father was a huge fan of Ava Gardner . . . you know, that actress with long, silky black hair from the fifties. He was sooo disappointed when I came out blonde-haired and blue-eyed."

"Well, I must say I was pretty taken by that blonde hair and those blue eyes last night," he said, trying to regain his composure.

His comment hung in the air like a cartoon strip bubble over his head. But when she said nothing, he rushed on, "Look, there's a band at the River Lounge tonight if you're interested. What'dya think?"

There was usually a party or bands playing around campus each weekend, and it was always the exact same . . . loud music, loud drunk people, and everyone looking to hook up. Inevitably early each morning after a party you could see girls sneaking out of the fraternity houses in their wrinkled clothes and mussed hair. They would jump into their car and speed away or scurry across campus back to their dorm room or sorority house before too many familiar faces could see them.

"I'm not really interested in seeing a band," she said.

Able slumped back in his chair and exhaled deeply. The dread started to build up and he felt the axe about to fall.

"I'd much rather just see you, Able."

He quickly sat back up and the rush of excitement made his cheeks flush. His heart beat out a tune that could rival any Conga band.

"Okay, great, uh, well," he stammered, trying to think faster than his brain would allow at the moment. "How about a nice dinner and maybe a drink afterward? That is . . . if you're not tired of me by then."

"That sounds splendid," she said in a fake high-brow accent. "And I'm sure I won't be tired of you . . . maybe I'll tire you out, though." She laughed her sexy laugh.

Who is this girl? Able thought. One minute she was "not that kind of girl," and then two seconds later she was a little sex kitten? He had no idea what to expect next or how to react. Able was experiencing a roller coaster of emotions and he usually hated roller coasters . . . but he kind of liked it this time. He decided to put his head down and plow forward.

"Okay, great, I'll pick you up around seven," he said with all the confidence he could muster. Which wasn't much.

"That sounds delightful," Ava said. "I'm in Coker Dorm at St. Margaret's. I'll meet you at the front entrance at seven."

"Yes, good, okay," Able said. "I'll see you at seven o'clock sharp, umm, bye."

Ava hung up the phone and Able stood there in a daze holding the receiver until "*if you'd like to make a call*" kicked in. What a dope.

Chapter Four

Able had a small, but rather intense panic attack as he turned off East Macon Street and made his way to Coker Dorm. The thought that he would soon be face-to-face again with Ava was almost more than his little male brain could bear. As each block passed, the lump in his throat seemed to grow larger and he began to feel a bit nauseated.

He drove a shit-brown 1972 Toyota Corolla station wagon that he had recently bought for $800. He called it the Millennium Falcon, Millie for short, as a tribute to his movie hero Han Solo. It was a fine little bucket of bolts, but it had two things wrong with it. It only had AM radio and. . .it ran only when it felt like running. He crossed his fingers each time he turned the key and hoped for the best.

Able pulled over to the side of the road just before the dorm's driveway to try to compose himself. He looked in the rearview mirror to make any necessary last-minute adjustments.

He smiled wide at the mirror to confirm that nothing was in his teeth. He breathed into his hands to check his breath. Yes, minty fresh, as advertised. Able scanned his freshly sun-kissed face in the rearview mirror for any rogue pimples. He ran his fingers through his long, brown hair to get the part just right. Nostrils flared for a routine booger check—good, no bears in the cave. Then he took a deep breath, ground the stick shift into first gear, and proceeded to Coker Dorm.

Able tried to muster as much confidence as possible, but deep down he knew who he really was—a nice, decent-looking kid with not too much to offer a girl who was so together and so beautiful. *What the hell*, he thought. Whatever happens at least I don't have Storm Troopers firing at me.

Ava was standing under the archway at the entrance of the dorm talking to another girl when Able arrived. He waved at her through the windshield, set the parking brake, and turned off the engine. He patted the dashboard and leaned in close to the steering wheel.

"Come on, Millie," he whispered. "Let's be a good girl tonight, okay?"

Then he got out and called out a "hello" that sounded more confident that he actually was.

"Hello, yourself," Ava responded with a smile.

Able walked around the car, took her hand, and leaned in to kiss her on the cheek. They did the ol' kiss-kiss hello thing. She continued to hold his hand, lightly swinging their arms and smiling. She was even more beautiful than he remembered as she stood there in the early evening light.

She wore a brown and black funky dress that hung loosely over her voluptuous figure. The dress came down to just above her knees, then transitioned to tall cowboy boots that he remembered from the night before. Her hair was flipped up every which way and teased to stick out perfectly in all directions, which enhanced her funky look. A small amount of makeup accentuated her lovely features . . . beautiful blue eyes, high cheekbones, full lips, and a great nose—not too small or wide and turned up ever so slightly. Able always thought it was the little things that really drew you to someone's look. A sexy mole, the way their nose scrunched when they laughed, things like that. Seriously, it was the little things that made you fall in love with someone, not the big picture. Ava had a monopoly on those lovable little things.

She wore a cameo necklace with a little photograph inside of her Grande, whom she adored. A gold chain hung around her long, smooth neck, and the cameo rested neatly between her lovely collar bones. She was smoking a clove cigarette—Able had never tried one, but he knew it was the "in" thing with the bohemian socially elite. He caught himself staring at Ava too long and quickly looked toward her friend and smiled.

"This is my best friend, Missy," Ava said. She turned to her friend. "Didn't fate ball bring me a completely adorable boy?"

"Yes, he's adorable all right," Missy answered with a grin. "I just hope he's worth it . . . fate ball or not."

Ava liked to refer to unexplained life events as "fate ball." You never know when or how fate ball will bounce into your life, she would say.

There was a short pause, and Able looked to Ava for some direction. She smiled a wry smile and laughed a guilty laugh.

"Nice to meet you, Able," Missy said as she quickly turned and walked back to the dorm. "I'll see y'all later."

They stood there for a moment with Ava swinging their arms back and forth.

"Well?" she said, raising her eyebrows with a "what next" look.

"Well," he repeated with a smile. Actually, he was still wondering about the "I hope he's worth it" comment, but he was too afraid to ask.

Able looked up and saw a bunch of girls peering out their dorm room windows waiting for something to happen. He recognized several as members of the Blonde Squad from the night before. He nodded a collective hello and smiled a nervous smile.

"If you're not going to say anything, then kiss her!" a girl yelled from above.

"Yeah, kiss her!" another shouted.

"Kiss her, kiss her, kiss her!" they began to chant.

Able looked at Ava with a "what the hell" shrug and leaned in for a kiss. But when he put his arms around her, she kissed him more passionately than he expected. He'd thought they would appease the girls with a simple smooch, but it quickly became wet and wild with a low dip for full effect. He pulled Ava upright again, then instinctively put a hand in his pocket. Ava's kiss had a bit more effect than just a gentle breeze.

"Wooo-hooo!" the girls cheered from the windows.

Able stepped back, faced the dorm, and with a low, sweeping bow, he acknowledged the crowd as if he had just sunk the winning putt at The Masters. He gave a few half bows as the cheers continued.

"You ready to go?" he asked, still in mid bow.

"Well," Ava said sheepishly. "There is a slight problem."

Able bolted to attention. His eyes filled with dread.

This was it. The jig was up. He was going to be exposed as the complete loser he knew himself to be. This whole thing was a ruse and the entire dorm was in on it. *Damn. How can women be so cruel,* he thought. He braced himself as he waited for Ava to plunge her hand into his chest and rip out his heart. She would hold it up high in the air, triumphant, and the dorm girls would cheer as he crumbled to the ground in a whimpering mass of maleness.

"A problem," he said, trying to not let his insecurities get the best of him.

"Well, a bunch of us got in trouble for missing curfew last night, and I was on thin ice with our house mother to begin with . . ." She paused and took a deep breath. "Anyway, the Mole, that's what we call our house mother—she kind of looks like a mole and is always digging around to catch us in something—well, she kinda caught me spray-painting the walls of the basement meeting room this afternoon."

"Spray paint, what were you doing with spray paint?" he asked. He wondered if she was with some secret girl-school-gang and she was out to get her colors—probably fuchsia, pink, or periwinkle.

Ava shuffled her feet and looked up at Able with a wry smile. It was the first time he'd seen her not exuding pure confidence. He could tell by the way she was acting that something was up. Their roles kind of reversed and he began to gain confidence by the second—not much confidence, mind you, but a little.

"I was, well, Missy and I were . . . writing on the walls with spray paint," she said, still shuffling her feet and looking at the ground.

"And you were writing . . ."

"Okay, okay, I was writing 'I love Able' all over the walls and making hearts and stuff." Her face turned a lovely pinkish red as the embarrassment welled up inside her. "But Missy did it, too," she said.

"So, Missy wrote 'I love Able' too?" he asked. "You know, I hardly even know the girl. I mean, I am charming and witty—and damn cute!—but really I just met her two minutes ago!"

Ava laughed and softly slapped him on the shoulder. "No, you nut, she was writing 'I love James,' a boy she met last night. Then the Mole appeared out of nowhere and busted us."

"Well," he said. "It sounds like either you're not a very sneaky graffiti artist, or she's a pretty good mole . . . maybe

it's a bit of both. So what's the problem?" He was feeling a little cocky given his new status as graffiti fodder. "A slap on the wrist, a hundred demerits, what?"

"We're campused," she said.

Able winced. *Campused* was a boarding-school term that he was not familiar with, but he got the idea.

"Well, I'm sorry you got caught," he said, giving Ava a consoling hug, "but I like the reason. No one has ever professed their love for me in spray paint before—certainly not after knowing me for fifteen minutes. You know, you should have spray-painted the side of an inner city building, or a highway overpass—I would have gotten a lot more press than graffiti spray-painted on the basement walls of an all-girls school, don't you think?"

"Shut up," Ava said with a laugh. "Look, we can still go out. You can go pick up some dinner and meet me under the large magnolia tree in the front corner of campus. Missy and I go there sometimes to ditch class or just talk. No one will know. It's very private with all the tree cover and bushes. I'll meet you there in like thirty minutes, okay?"

Able didn't really care if the date was in a fancy restaurant or a ditch; he just wanted to spend more time with her. She made him feel so good and so comfortable. Plus she was the prettiest girl who'd ever voluntarily talked to him. Even though she was this incredibly beautiful girl, he felt like he belonged beside her. Normally, Able wouldn't feel worthy of being in the presence of such beauty. He usually left that up to the pretty-boy jocks that seemed to *never* have trouble with the ladies, but this time was different. This time it felt natural.

"Okay," he said, turning toward the car. "I'll see you in a little bit with a feast fit for a king, or ah, a queen."

Ava didn't let go of his hand, but pulled him back to her with an unexpected jerk. She held both his hands and faced him.

"You can never leave without kissing me goodbye," she said with a grin. "That's my number-one rule."

"Well," Able said, "I'm a real stickler for following rules. You can ask anyone who knows me, and they'll tell you that I am a rule-following-fool. Yes sir, rules are meant to be followed, and follow your rule I will—"

Ava put her index finger over his mouth. "Shut up and kiss me, Mr. Rule Follower." She gave him a long goodbye kiss that would have to hold him until they met at the magnolia tree.

Chapter Five

The *clump, clump, clump* of Ava's cowboy boots hitting metal echoed in the stairwell and rang in her ears as she ran down the hallway and into her dorm room.

She pulled the duvet cover off her bed, grabbed several pillows, and put two large candles and a lighter in her back pack. She walked to the bathroom down the hall, which was shared by the twenty girls on her floor. It had only five showers, five toilets, and five sinks with mirrors, which usually led to estrogen overload on those nights when all the girls were getting ready for parties or dates at the same time.

But at the moment, Ava had the bathroom to herself. She unlocked her locker and grabbed her toothbrush and toothpaste. She eyed the box of tampons for a good ten seconds and bit her lower lip. She wondered if she could do without this time.

The bathroom door swung open and Somer Albright strolled in. She looked impeccable in a little black outfit with cute black strappy pumps. She wore single diamond earrings and a single diamond necklace that hung just below the nape of her tanned neck. Somer was the classic St. Margaret's rich bitch, who didn't like Ava at all, since she considered her to be her stiffest competition for male attention. Somer was from Charleston and drove a black Mercedes convertible, which looked smashing wrapped around her, especially when she wore black. She was thin, flat chested enough to not require a bra, dirty blonde, and very pretty. She envied Ava's curves, her perfect skin, and her natural allure to the opposite sex.

"You look pretty tonight," said Ava, trying to be nice as she squeezed toothpaste onto her purple, ergonomically correct toothbrush. "Hot date?"

"Of course," Somer said in her natural bitchy tone. "What gave it away, Einstein?"

Ava smiled politely, trying not to be sucked in by Somer's taunt. "Me too," said Ava as she began to brush her teeth.

"When you're a slut," Somer said very matter-of-factly, now applying blush to her cheeks, "it's not called a date, it's called turning a trick."

"Fruck yeww," said Ava turning to Somer with a mouth full of toothpaste. Toothpaste foam flew onto the mirror and a few little foam droplets splattered on Somer. The girl quickly wiped the little specks off her arm and cheek, then turned to Ava.

"Not tonight," said Somer as she began to put her makeup away in a small greenish blue Chanel bag. "I'm saving this vagina for someone special, unlike you who gives it away to every Tom, Dick, and dick."

Somer cocked her head to the side when she said this, then flipped her hair back as she passed Ava. "Toodles!" she said as she exited the bathroom with her two-inch heels making a *click, click, click* sound across the tile floor.

Ava was alone again. She looked down at her hand holding the toothbrush and it trembled uncontrollably. That was all the proof she needed.

Ava went back to her locker and got out the box of tampons. She pulled out two mini bottles of vodka, then went to the nearest stall and locked the door. She twisted the cap off one bottle, threw her head back, and sucked it dry in no time. She tossed the empty into the toilet and flushed. The little bottle swirled around and around in the mini whirlpool for a few seconds, then disappeared with a glug. Ava twisted the cap of the second bottle and sucked it down fast, then flushed the empty.

Ava walked over to the vanity and stared at herself in the mirror. The alcohol felt warm as it made its way through her veins. She closed her eyes and concentrated on that warm feeling for a moment. She thought of Able and a smile curled across her lips. She really did like this boy. There was something about him that was different, but she didn't quite know what it was just yet. She pinched her cheeks for color, took a swig of mouth wash, then returned to her room, grabbed her supplies, and headed across campus to the magnolia tree.

Chapter Six

Able parked the car on the street just down from campus so as not to create any suspicion. Although jumping over the front brick wall with a backpack probably blew his cover. He acted as if he were in some double secret covert operation. He hid behind trees, crouched behind bushes, and slinked around campus, even though most likely nobody knew or cared about their rendezvous except the two of them.

The sun wasn't quite down to the horizon yet, but the moon was already up. A gentle breeze drifted through campus and sent the leaves into a slow dance. It was one of those incredible early fall evenings that make you feel good about living in the South. In twenty-four hours the weather turned from unbearable to unbelievable.

Able's eye was drawn to a quaint little white chapel on the edge of campus sitting off by itself. It was where they held Episcopal services every Sunday for those "boarders" really

interested in God and also for those who only needed to repent and cleanse their souls after a Saturday night of debauchery. The whole concept of repentance was a wonderful thing, Able thought. It has saved many from eternal damnation, or at least postponed it for a while, anyway.

Able's mother always told him he was a sensitive boy. He understood what she meant when his mind began to wander, and for the first time ever he fantasized about his wedding day with friends and family in this very spot.

Ava and Able walk out of the little white chapel all smiles and are immediately pelted by a blizzard of rice. Bette Midler's version of "Going to the Chapel" plays over the loudspeakers. Everyone is dancing out of the chapel and having a grand old time. They get into a mint 1957 Jaguar convertible as their guests surround the car clapping and cheering. His groomsmen have tied the requisite cans to the bumper of their getaway car below the "Just Married" sign. They wave to the crowd as he shifts into first gear. He turns to kiss his new bride and . . .

"Able!" Ava called quietly from under the large magnolia tree. "Able, over here." She lifted up one of the large lower branches and motioned with her other hand.

"What were you doing over there?" she asked as he approached.

"Oh, nothing," he said as he slid under the branch and

crawled to a comfortable spot. "Just thinking about kissing you again, that's all."

Ava smiled. She placed her hand on the back of his neck and said, "You can kiss me anytime, darlin'." She pulled him in for a short, passionate kiss.

The magnolia tree was the perfect spot with just enough room to sit up straight without banging your head on a limb. It was secluded enough to elude the most gung-ho security guard . . . or Mole. Ava had prepared the area with a large, soft duvet cover and a few colorful pillows. Near the trunk of the tree, she'd arranged several candles that glowed brightly and added a romantic touch to their little love nest. He opened his backpack and pulled out a bottle of red wine and two Steak Jr.s with fries from The Grill, an old-time burger joint that was a town favorite. He'd considered Chinese food, but didn't want to guess if Ava was sweet and sour or hot and spicy. Italian food was too messy with the possibility of marinara sauce flying everywhere with each slurp of a noodle. So he decided on the all-American hamburger and fries from a fifties retro diner. He figured it couldn't miss.

"Oh my God!" Ava said, all excited. "You read my mind."

"I did?" Able said, a bit puzzled. "Well then, I better get these pants off." He tugged at his pants and made noise like the Three Stooges to give it the full effect, "huummff,

ahhhh, eeehhhh." Able was not above being an idiot for love, or at least lust for the moment.

"No, you nut," she said with a laugh. "I love The Grill. It's totally my favorite place to eat in town. Darlin', you have made me very happy."

They sat under the magnolia tree, ate dinner, and talked about every topic under the sun. They goofed off and laughed between bites of their Steak Jr.s. They fed each other French fries and even did the wrap-around-and-feed yourself thing that usually required champagne, but fries did well in a pinch. Ava became very playful and stuck a fry up Able's nose, which sent them into the silly giggles. Of course, he let it stay in there for a few minutes like nothing was wrong, which was hilarious. They took turns washing the feast down with swigs of red wine straight from the bottle until it was empty.

Able thought there was nothing quite like seeing a beautiful girl take a swig of wine straight from the bottle and wipe her mouth with her sleeve. Man, that was sexy. It's sexy like a beautiful girl driving an old pickup truck, or when you see a woman in a power moment. Like when a woman boss gives her male subordinates hell for missing a deadline or something, and she leans on the conference table to really make her point while showing nice cleavage. It's an "I can fire you today, but you'll still want me tonight" kind of power play. Able knew Ava had a power over him.

Ava and Able lay back on the duvet cover and watched the candlelight reflect off the underside of the large magnolia leaves. Shadows danced around their little love fort as the leaves swayed in the breeze. Ava lay against him with her head on his shoulder. They held hands and talked, occasionally turning toward each other to kiss, to caress a cheek, or just to stare into each other's eyes in the flickering candlelight. Happiness and contentment engulfed them. It was as if they'd known each other for years instead of just a few hours. Able had never felt so comfortable with a woman, any woman—even his mother—and that was saying something, since she changed his diapers and all.

"I'm sorry I jumped you last night," Ava said as he held her close. "I hope it didn't give you the wrong impression."

"Well, I'm not sorry," he said. "Because I never would have approached you in a million years. Oh, I would have watched you from across the room and wondered what it would take for me to be with someone as wonderful as you, but I never would have made a move."

"Why not?" she asked, propping herself up on one elbow and turning to look him in the eye. "You're adorable and funny and smart . . . that's what girls want, not some asshole pretty boy." She sounded sincere, but his experience told him that stunningly beautiful women and adorable, sweet guys just didn't last.

"Let me just enjoy you for as long as possible," he said. He gently caressed her cheek and looked deep into her baby blues. "And I hope that's a long, long time."

Able pulled Ava on top of him and kissed her with more passion than he ever thought possible. He felt a connection with this girl . . . a connection that he had never felt before. It wasn't just her being beautiful, or cool, or the fact that she performed a tonsillectomy on him last night. She needed him . . . he felt like for some reason she needed him . . . and now he needed her, too.

Able reached for the duvet cover and pulled it over both of them. They snuggled together under the covers and smooched and hugged and hugged and smooched. He held her tightly against his body and closed his eyes. He could feel her heart beat against his chest and he breathed in her sweet scent. Able took her face in his hands and kissed her with meaning. They held each other close and slowly drifted off to sleep.

Able woke up to rays of sunlight creeping through the thick blanket of magnolia leaves. For a moment, he couldn't make sense of where he was. He glanced at his watch. It was seven in the morning.

Then he turned his head and remembered.

Ava. Sleeping beside him. More beautiful than any dream.

She was wrapped up in the duvet cover, and it framed her perfectly angelic face. He leaned down and kissed her temple once . . . twice . . . three times. With each kiss he pressed his lips to her skin a bit longer than the time before, and with each kiss a surge of emotion filled his body.

As he lay there and admired her beauty, Able knew she was too good to be true. *No one could be this beautiful and this perfect and fall for me,* he thought. He had never met a person who didn't have something wrong with them–living a secret life, being a serial killer, having a pimple, for God's sake . . . something! He had a feeling that falling for Ava was not the most emotionally responsible decision he could make, but he was already in mid tumble. Able was allowing himself to fall, although he knew it was really just a matter of time until the day would come when she would kick the shit out of him and move on to someone better.

Her eyes slowly opened. "Good morning, darlin'," she said. She reached up and ran her fingers through his hair. "I need a kiss."

They kissed for a moment. Just a few quick pecks, though, in case either one of them had bad morning breath. It's awful when you wake up with someone who wants to really kiss—like French kiss—before they even brush their teeth. You hate to even think about it, but you know it happens every day of the year.

"Well, it looks like we missed curfew," he said softly. "I think we're both in trouble this time."

"Then can you snuggle with me for a while longer?" she said as she got cozy and nuzzled his shoulder. "I may not be able to leave my dorm room for a few days, since the Mole is probably waiting in the lobby ready to put me in lockdown."

Able wasn't too eager to get home and confront his mother, either. Even though he was nineteen, he wasn't allowed to stay out all night long. Plus, there was no better place in the world to be at that very moment than in the arms of a beautiful woman who wanted him.

So they continued to lie there under the magnolia tree and added a few more hours to the world's most perfect date.

Chapter Seven

It turned out the Mole was waiting for Ava in the lobby and she was put on lock down . . . for three whole days. She was only allowed to go to class or the dining hall and then it was straight back to her dorm room. No visitors, no roaming the campus and certainly no leaving the school grounds. It was one of those times when it just sucked to be young and not in control of your own life.

There was the phone, however, so they talked several times every day about nothing in particular. It made Able feel good just to know that she was on the other end of the line and wanted to see him again. He was sure his so-called charm would have worn thin by now.

"I made you something in art class today," Ava said. "You should get it in the mail tomorrow."

He pictured her lying on her unmade bed wearing wrinkled, paint-splattered art class clothes and tussled hair.

He could picture her smiling as they spoke and he longed to touch her. Able debated in his head about asking her to have phone sex, but his brain decided that you should have done more than just kiss, however passionately, before stepping over that sexual land mine.

"What did you make me?"

"Not tellin'," she said. "It's a surprise."

"C'mon," he whined.

"Nope."

"Please."

"No, no, no, no, no, no," she sang with a giggle.

"All right, but it better be good."

"Darlin'," she said in her sexiest voice. "If it's from me you know it's good."

They both laughed and talked about nothing in particular for a while longer until the Mole knocked on her door. "Lights out!" she barked.

The next day a package arrived at his parents' house. Able's mother called to him from the kitchen and he ran down to see what it was. The package was tattooed with big red lips, hearts and little sayings here and there, like "spank this" and "kiss me."

It was addressed to "The delicious Able Curran," and a drawing of an apple with a bite taken out of it was just to the left of the address. The sender's artistic wrapping did not escape his mother's eye, although the symbolism of the apple did escape him at that moment. After years of being an acolyte, singing in the youth choir and pretty much being force fed Christianity, Able had come to appreciate the plight of Adam in the Garden of Eden. If any man today were in that same predicament you know he would have taken the bite too. I mean, when a hot, naked woman tells you to bite something, dammit, you bite it . . . and hard.

"So," his mother said in a disapproving voice, "who's the ar-teest." She could not have been more sarcastic. She handed him the package as she spoke, but would not let go of her end.

"Just a girl I know," he said, as he tugged on the package.

"Uh huh," replied his mother, "and what kind of girl sends a package like this to a young man? A girl who's trouble, that's who."

His mother was always asking, then answering her own questions. That's why she was always right. She could have a whole conversation with herself, even a fight depending on the subject matter, and no one had to say a word. All Able needed to do was just nod his head once in a while and she would take care of the rest.

"With the package marked up the way it is on the outside," she said beginning to gesture wildly with her one free hand. "There's no telling what's inside this thing. It's probably far worse . . . something crude I'm sure . . . maybe even pornographic!"

"Mom," he tried to interrupt, but she was on a roll.

"You had better not bring any pornographic material into this house young man! Do you hear me?"

"Mom."

"I want you to tell this, this, this girl that you want nothing to do with her sick little mind."

"Mom!" Able yelled loud enough to put her on pause. "Take it easy. This is a very nice girl who just has a little sassiness in her personality. She's being funny. It's a joke."

"I would never have sent a package like this to a boy when I was a young girl," she said disgustedly. "No girl would have sent a package like that in my day, well, maybe Sally Gordon, but she was trashy anyway . . ."

"Mom!" he yelled again. He had to nip it in the bud or she would go on about her "growing up years" for hours. "Mom, we live in a different world now than from a hundred years ago. Girls can be more forward and it's not trashy." She hated how he referred to her youth as "a hundred years ago." She was only fifty, but it made for good theatrics and it usually got her laughing.

"You know good and well I'm not that old," she said, finally getting down from her high horse.

"Look, Mom," he said jokingly, "go take out your teeth, soak your feet and relax. I'll come back later and spoon feed you some gruel."

"Oh, hush," she said, as she slapped at his shoulder. She shooed Able out of the kitchen. "Go on now, get going, I've got things to do." She paused for a second, then said, "If I find any pornography when I clean your room you'll be in big trouble, young man!"

Able ran upstairs and jumped on his bed. He sat there studying the package and laughed out loud at the drawings and writings. *The delicious Able Curran,* he said to himself with a laugh. *That's awesome.*

He opened the package and several items spilled out onto his bed. There was a cone and leaf from their magnolia tree; a small pad of sticky notes with little sayings written on them, like "I'm thinking of you, A" and "Kiss me now, A" with instructions to place them strategically in his room, car or locker at work; and finally a small watercolor painting of a tree with long, swooping branches and a light purple sky with just the hint of a peach-colored setting sun. There was a note on the back of the painting that read:

"Close your eyes, think of me as we kiss beneath this lovely tree."

Signed "A."

He couldn't stop smiling. Able had never received a package quite like this one.

Chapter Eight

The lock-down time dragged by as slow as molasses. Able was going crazy not being able to see Ava. When the three days finally ended he could hardly contain himself. Really, he was busting at the seams—smiling and giggling like a little school girl. It was really kind of pathetic, but that's love. To celebrate her release from Mole prison, Ava and Able went to a local watering hole called Harrison's Bar. They met Missy and her new boyfriend James for a few drinks and a night on the town. It turned out that James was a buddy of Able's and they just happened to hook up with two best friends. It had to be a first—two of the prettiest girls in town dating two of the biggest dopes in town—nice, sweet dopes mind you, but dopes nonetheless.

They slid into a corner booth, ordered the first of several pitchers of beer and laughed and talked for hours. Harrison's Bar was dark and loud with pool tables in

the back room and a Galaga video game in the corner. The standard neon beer signs were placed strategically around the bar. A largemouth bass hung on one wall and a large buck was displayed behind the bar. Inevitably, there would be at least one wise guy each night who would use the "nice rack" line on a girl at the bar, then point to the buck when she looked all disgusted. Able never used that line himself, but it always cracked him up. The "nice rack" line never actually worked, but it produced a few grins and a couple of slaps, for sure. Guys will try anything to get into a girls shirt, they really will. Most guys have begged and pleaded for just a peek. Boys are just hard-wired to crave bosoms. It must start with breast feeding when they're little babies and never really goes away. Anyway, all guys must have it–at least when they're nineteen years old with raging hormones.

Harrison's was mainly a hang-out for all the kids from the nearby colleges, but a few old bar flies always seemed to be there talking politics or sports. It was a fun place for young folks to drink, hang out and shoot pool to start out their evening. Later on, most everybody would go dancing at a place down the street called the Culture Club, which was the disco of the day with strobe lights and smoke machines. Finally, at around three in the morning everyone would stumble back to their dorm rooms or apartments. It was very convenient for the drunk college kids to have everything so close. Surely, it's just what their parents had in mind when they sent little Johnny off to school at $15,000 a year, plus books and board.

Harrison's was always crowded late on the weekend and there always seemed to be several people Able knew, or at least recognized from partying around town. Every now and then he'd run into a girl with whom he made out before. He would struggle to remember her name–not that he didn't care—he's just really bad with names. It was a little embarrassing to see those girls, especially if it was one of the girls who he begged for a peek. It seemed like most guys lose their self-respect when there's the slightest possibility of seeing a nipple.

It wasn't quite as uncomfortable when he ran into one of the girls who actually showed him something. At least they hadn't seen him down on his knees begging for a peek like a complete dope. Of course, the list of girls who actually gave him a peek was pretty small and the girls who actually unleashed their bosoms for his benefit was smaller still. Able never really thought much about getting into a girl's pants just because it seemed so unattainable. And actual sex, man, that was just pure fantasy in his mind. So, he concentrated above the belly button, since the odds of sexual success were much better.

James, Missy, Ava and Able played quarters between never-serious conversations—gossip about people

around town, upcoming concerts and the drudgery of school, who's a bitch, who's a bastard—you know, nineteen-year-old type stuff. They laughed constantly. He had never smiled and laughed so much in his life. All they ever seemed to do was smile and laugh, laugh and smile, oh yeah . . . and fool around . . . can't forget the fooling around–that was the best part.

James aimed carefully at the glass, then bounced the quarter off the table only to have it ding against the rim of the glass and fall on the table with a wobble, wobble, wobble until it rested in a pool of spilled beer.

"Oh, dee-nied," James said in apparent agony.

"Drink yuh soarry bastard!" said Able with an exaggerated English accent. "Yuh betta work on yuh game, boy, or yuh be floatin' outta here."

Sometimes Able would talk in different accents just for the fun of it. Maybe it was easier to say things in a made up accent, because it wasn't really him saying it. Sometimes it was just a goof, but other times it was really covering his butt. Able began to think, *I know they think I'm crazy and maybe I am. I swear, I could probably buy a shrink a beach house if I ever started going to one. I'm not too messed up though—no more than anyone else anyway.*

James chugged his beer and slammed the empty mug on the table with a loud "aaahhhh" and wiped his mouth with his sleeve. They'd already gone through two pitchers and were feeling no pain.

"Bar maid!" he yelled holding up the empty pitcher as their waitress walked by, "another pitcher . . . no, make that two pitchers, plleeaassee."

James was a goofy kid, but in a funny kind of way. He was always trying to crack a joke or pretend to get hit in the nose by an opening door. One time he poured a whole pitcher of beer over his head just to get a girl to kiss him. He looked like a wet rat, but she laid one on him good anyway. Physical comedy was his true calling, but his parents had a more profitable future mapped out for him. They were both doctors and expected him to be a doctor too—end of discussion.

Some of the tight-ass guys they usually hung out with saw his antics as kind of geeky, but the girls loved it. Men will do anything to attract women and James was a goddamn chick magnet with his silly antics. He didn't care how stupid he looked, if the girls laughed that was all that mattered and he kept them in stitches.

They all laughed, partly from James' silliness, partly from being tipsy and partly from all being giddy with love. You could see it in their eyes and feel it in their energy. They were all smiling, all the time, even when there was complete silence. They would all just sit and smile and touch and kiss, and then smile some more. They were sure they drove the people around them nuts, but they really didn't care. People are usually jealous of what they don't have. Oh, they put on a good face and say things like, "I'm sooo happy for you," like at a wedding or something, but they're really burning up with jealousy inside.

James pounded his fist on the table to get everyone's attention. "All right," he said, puckering his lips and making a smooching noise, "who needs some sugar?" He was always trying to get their attention to make some grand announcement or something, but the announcements were never really that grand. Usually he just wanted them to hear his joke or watch him goof.

Able raised his hand real high like he was in the back of a classroom and had the perfect answer. He said that he needed some sugar and reached across the table and grabbed James's face with both hands. Able kissed him on the cheek with a loud "SMACK." Of course, the girls laughed like it was the funniest thing they'd ever seen.

"Not what I was thinking, my friend," James said wiping his cheek with his hand. "I prefer girl cooties." He turned to Missy and said, "give me some of *those* cooties, baby." She leaned in and kissed him pretty good.

"Well, I want some of those cooties," said Ava pointing at Able from six inches away. She placed a finger under his chin and turned his head towards her to line up their lips. They kissed long and passionately. She was so sexy that sometimes he would just get totally lost and forget where he was when they were kissing. Ava never really cared too much if others saw them kissing or doing whatever, she was pure confidence. Man, did she have power.

"Okay, okay," said James after watching them kiss for a full minute, "let's break it up kids . . . there IS a time limit on PDA and your time be up." They stopped kissing and Ava reached over and used her thumb to wipe his mouth since they really got into it a little bit. It wasn't a big deal though, not really.

It was nearly two o'clock in the morning and the overhead lights flickered on and off just like every night at that time. "Last call!" shouted the bartender. "Let's finish 'em up people!"

They had been talking and drinking and laughing for hours. The time flew by and no one really wanted to leave. Ava and Missy had gotten weekend passes to go home, but, of course, it was just another ruse. Able had told his parents that he was staying with James and James told his parents he was staying with Able, so all of them were covered. They were all good kids and their parents trusted them completely, so they could take advantage of them pretty easily once in a blue moon. They knew they couldn't take advantage of that kind of blind trust

too often or they'd get busted and lose it for good. A lot of parents think they know everything about their kids, but most of them don't know pea-turkey. Kids are sneakier than most parents know—at least some of them are—and sometimes parents don't find out what's really going on until the cops show up at the front door.

When Able was about twelve his best friend Alfred and he each stole a bunch of eggs from their mothers' refrigerators. They went down to this girl's house who was always really mean to them. It was Halloween night and they had been planning their little caper for a week. They dressed up like pirates thinking the patch over one eye, a scarf on their heads and a charcoal beard would be a good disguise. They trick-or-treated like everyone else until they got around to the mean girl's house. They hid in the bushes until the coast was clear of ghosts, witches, princesses and hobos. Then they rained farm-fresh eggs all over her brick, ranch style house. It was like a flock of chickens were flying over head and all decided to lay at the same time. Pop, pop, pop, pop, pop!

They ran off down the street and dove behind the hedge at Mrs. Coble's house to hide. They lay on their backs and tried to catch their breath.

"Did you connect?" Alfred asked huffing and puffing.

"Hell yeah," Able said gasping for air, "about six damn times."

"Me too," he said. "Man, we got her good."

They both went home after trick-or-treating some more like nothing had happened. Able ate his allotted few pieces of candy, washed off his pirate beard and went off to bed. His father came into his room at about ten o'clock and said he had some visitors downstairs. No way, he thought, who would visit a twelve year old so late. He went downstairs to find two policemen at the front door. Turns out his little tattle tale neighbor saw him with a shirt-full of eggs and mentioned it to his father. He put two and two together and called the cops on Able. Able couldn't believe it. His own father called the cops on him just for egging a house—and the house of a snotty bitch, no less. Anyway, he learned his lesson and never egged another house. It took years to regain the blind trust of his parents again, but they came around eventually.

Missy, James, Ava and Able all sat there thinking of what to do next. Of course, there was always the Rose Garden for a marathon make-out session, or going to a late night party at someone's apartment since there was always a late night somewhere, or they could go to the IHOP for breakfast. None of the standard options really excited them too much.

"I want to see the sunrise," said Ava real excited.

"Yeah, let's stay up and watch the sunrise," Missy agreed. "It will be beautiful coming up over that meadow near the fair grounds."

Their other late-night option was going up to the fields near the fairgrounds and mess with the cows. It sounds stupid, but it was usually a pretty fun time. They never hurt them or anything–no cow tipping or nothing–they just mooed at them and yelled things like "get the grill" or maybe they'd snap a beer bottle cap in their direction. Very tame stuff like that.

"I'd rather see the sunrise over the ocean," said Ava. "That would really be beautiful. Then we could play on the beach all day."

James and Able looked at each other with a nod of approval, then looked at the girls and smiled. "Beach me," said James pointing at himself with both thumbs extended. He had little gestures like that for everything.

"We're two hours from my grandmother's cottage," Able said. "It's right on the beach."

"Do you have a key?" asked James.

"Key shmee," he said, "we'll just break in, it's easy."

Their family beach cottage was shared by four families, who had produced way too many grandchildren. It was common knowledge among the older grandchildren that one window lock was broken and if you could get up on the porch roof, it was a cinch to get in the cottage. His older cousins had been breaking in for years and they recently passed this knowledge down to the younger generation.

And a sacred tradition continued.

Chapter Nine

Charleston, South Carolina

—February 1994—

"I really think I should go alone," said Able as he poured two glasses of red wine. "I appreciate your offering to come with me, June, but this is something I need to do by myself."

He handed his wife a glass of her favorite Pinot Noir and they strolled out to the side, screened-in porch. They watched Maggie and a neighbor's child clinging to the rope swing that hung from a large oak tree. They giggled and screamed as the swing untwisted and spun them both quickly into dizziness.

"Okay, honey," said June in her understanding tone. "If you think it's best."

"I do," he said as he walked over and wrapped his arms around her. "I love you so much, sweetie."

Able kissed his loving wife goodbye and called out to Maggie. "I'll be back in time to kiss you goodnight," he shouted through cupped hands. "Love you!" Maggie waved with a fully extended arm to make sure he saw her, then blew rapid fire kisses his way as Able strolled to the car.

The visitation was held at the Dubose home in Mount Pleasant. It was a short drive across the bridge from Charleston, but it felt like an eternity to Able as he navigated the traffic and his emotions. The Dubose house was beautiful and dated back to the late 1800s. The gated semi-circle driveway was lined with two hundred-year-old English boxwoods and Spanish moss dripping from the live oaks. The entry to the house had wide steps that lead to a grand front porch that wrapped around the right side and connected with an even larger back porch overlooking the sound. The back yard was large enough to accommodate two large tents for the fully catered affair. The Dubose family never did anything low key and the visitation for their eldest daughter's death was no different. A piano player set the mood inside with upbeat tunes, but not too upbeat. The full band in the back yard was under one tent and kept the mourners in a more festive mood as they mingled out back and on the pier that stretched two hundred feet over the marsh and into the sound.

Able avoided the receiving line at the front door and made his way around back to one of the many bars at the event. He ordered a bourbon on the rocks, waded through the crowd on the back porch, then made his way inside. He didn't know half of the people and he was sure many didn't know Ava. Most were friends of her parents lending their support, or enjoying another exquisite Dubose spread. Able nodded often as he made his way through the crowd of unfamiliar faces.

"Oh my God, Able!" said a woman as he approached. "Is that you?"

"I think so," said Able. "And you are?"

"Has it been so fucking long that you don't even recognize me?" she said. "Missy, it's me, Missy." She threw her arms around Able and hugged him tightly.

"Missy," he said with a smile. "I can't believe it. You look incredible."

"Don't be so shocked, Able," she said with a laugh as she stepped back. "All this costs a shit-load of money." She framed her face with her hands acknowledging the plastic surgery from years ago, then cupped both of her breasts. "And these, too," she said. "I was always so envious of Ava's chest and now I have my own."

"Well, you look wonderful," said Able. "How's James?

We haven't talked in years."

"I don't know and I couldn't care less," said Missy matter-of-factly. "We haven't talked in years either."

"I'm sorry. I didn't realize you split up."

Missy and Able caught up on their lives. Missy couldn't get pregnant and eventually she and James grew apart. Once divorced, she decided to "fix" all those things that she wanted . . . a smaller nose, bigger breasts, less-flabby thighs. She had been playing the singles game again after many years of marriage and she was enjoying herself.

"Maybe Ava can do me one last favor and get me laid tonight," said Missy in a whisper. "There is some nice young talent here."

"Good luck with that," said Able. "Great to see you again. I'm going to find the family before it gets too late."

The old friends hugged goodbye. Able walked toward the front of the house and Missy headed out back to troll the dance floor.

Able stopped in his tracks when he saw the Dubose family all in a line, still greeting visitors near the front door. Mr. and Mrs. Dubose had aged quite a bit, but they both still looked like Southern royalty. Lovey was tall, thin, blonde and beautiful as ever. She was the good daughter who never strayed and did everything by the book.

His heart thumped quickly in his chest and he dabbed the sweat off his forehead with his cocktail napkin. He tossed back his bourbon, then took a deep breath before he made his way closer.

Lovey was the first to see him approaching. She quickly excused herself from a guest and pushed through the crowd. She threw her arms around Able's neck and began to weep for the first time that night.

"Oh, Able," she said through her sobs. "You are so wonderful to be here. I can't thank you enough . . . all these years . . . you were always there for her . . . she loved you so much. I want you to know that she loved you so, so much."

Able didn't say a word, but held onto Lovey tightly as tears rolled down his cheeks. The reality of her being gone struck him again and he simply wept. Mr. and Mrs. Dubose were called over by Lovey and they all surrounded Able. The crowd parted as if for a spotlight dance and encircled the four whose lives were forever entwined by their love for a long-lost soul.

"You were so good to her," said Mrs. Dubose as she spoke softly into Able's ear. "Thank you for loving my Ava. We all love you, Able. You are such a good man."

Mr. Dubose stepped forward and hugged his wife and Able at the same time. His eyes were filled with tears as he fought to be the tough but tender father that was his reputation. He looked Able in the eye, shook his hand and then pulled him in for a hug. Mr. Dubose rarely hugged anyone . . . especially another man.

"Thank you, Able," he said sternly, trying to hold back his emotions. "Thank you for everything."

Mr. Dubose couldn't hold back anymore. He squeezed Able tightly and the dam burst. Able became the consoler again and let the man who never showed any emotion cry like a baby on his shoulder. After a full minute Mr. Dubose stood up straight, wiped his eyes, lovingly patted Able on the cheek, took a deep breath, then returned to socialize with the crowd.

Able gave a last hug to Mrs. Dubose and Lovey. They expressed their deep appreciation for him again, then he slipped away and disappeared into the crowd.

Chapter Ten

Savannah, Georgia

—September 1980—

James' car was a late model BMW 320i with pale blue exterior and tan interior . . . a real sweet ride. James set the cruise control at sixty-five as they cruised down the lonely highway toward the coast. The stereo was turned up loud and The Who's "My Generation" screamed out of the speakers. James did his best Keith Moon impression thumping the steering wheel to the beat, while Able performed a Pete Townsend abbreviated windmill stroke in the small back seat. As with any successful road trip they had a good mix-tape of classic rock songs and pushed the stereo's speakers to the edge. Able didn't know why they put numbers on the volume control, it should just say loud, louder and loudest. They played the music on the loudest setting, so any conversation was worthless, unless they screamed at the top of their lungs.

Early into the trip they pulled into an all-night convenience store to pick up some supplies. The girls got cigarettes, gum and bottled water—very girly stuff for a road trip, Able thought. He and James stocked-up on the real road trip essentials . . . Moon Pies and Pepsi, roasted peanuts, M&Ms and a box of Cracker Jacks. Able picked up a large orange juice and some Sweet Sixteen doughnuts for breakfast and hoped they would last until morning.

They drove down the highway listening to music and singing. If they didn't know the words they faked it, which was most of the time. They danced with their arms flailing about and bounced up and down on the seats like a bunch of kids at Gymboree. They had a great time.

After a while, Ava and Able hunkered down in the back seat. He balled up his high school letterman's jacket and used it as a cushion against the window. Ava leaned back against him and lay her head on his chest nuzzling him until she found just the right spot. He kissed her sweetly on the forehead before they closed their eyes and drifted off to sleep.

Able never really fell totally asleep though, but just lay there with his eyes closed. He started thinking about where he was and how he had gotten to this place. How did he meet this amazing girl with such beauty and style? He had never been this happy before in his life. He figured that this must be what pure happiness felt like.

He liked pure happiness . . . who wouldn't . . . it's pure happiness for God's sake. He kissed Ava on the forehead again and breathed in deeply. She smelled so good . . . a mix of clove cigarettes, Chanel #5, hairspray and baby powder. It sounded like a strange mixture of scents, but the combination was brilliant. She made him feel like there was no better place to be at that moment in the world than screaming down a dark and lonely highway in a powder blue B'mer with the girl of his dreams in his arms. *Corny*, he thought, *but true*.

"Hey, Able, get up," James called quietly. "I need a navigator."

His moment of pure happiness was quickly interrupted, so he opened his eyes and looked out the window. One of his favorite songs, Meatloaf's "Paradise (by the dashboard light)," spilled out of the stereo. He could hear it easily, but it wasn't blaring out of the speakers like the earlier songs. It was pitch black outside and the lights of the city twinkled far in the distance.

Able got his bearings and then gave simple directions to James. "Keep going straight until you cross the bridge," he said in his gruff early morning voice. "Then turn left at the yacht basin."

"Turn left where?" James asked.

"The yacht basin," he said.

"The Yack Base Inn?"

"Where all the boats are, you dumb ass," barked Able.

"Easy there, cowboy," said James. "If you'd use that private school education and enunciate once in a while, then maybe I could understand what the hell you're saying."

"Yeah," Able said sarcastically. "You really think there's a Yack Base Inn? You're an idiot."

"Shut up," James said.

"You shut up."

Every now and then they would have this kind of intelligent banter that lasted all of thirty seconds. They weren't really being mean, just trying to be funny with kind of a mean edge. It was kind of like when boys trashed their friend's mother.

They turned left where all the boats were and drove the few blocks through town toward the cottage. The streets were eerily empty. Neon motel signs flickered "VACANCY" against the dark night sky of early fall. A red neck drove by in his tweaked out pick'em up truck with thumping base so loud that it tickled their inner ears. A miniature "Stars and Bars" confederate flag flapped wildly from the antennae and a sticker that read "Southern Pride" adorned the rear windshield. Rednecks are a special breed of human who are unique to America. Our little gift to the world.

They pulled up to the cottage, woke the girls and all climbed out of the car stretching and yawning loudly. The thick, salt air filled Able's senses and the crash of the waves in the distance was music to his ears. He had always loved the beach and could sit and watch the waves for hours. He took Ava by the hand and walked up the stairs and along the wrap-around porch, then down the boardwalk to the moonlit sand. He stood behind Ava and draped his arms over her shoulders and hugged her tightly. They looked out at the ocean and took in the beauty of 5:00 a.m. along Saint Simons Island on the Georgia coastline. The moonlight glistened on the water and danced on the waves. A light breeze blew off the ocean and made being out on the beach a bit chilly. They sat in the cool sand and took off their shoes and socks. Able rolled up his pants and walked down to the water. Hermit crabs darted back into their holes for safety. The dry sand felt cool on his bare feet and the wet sand at the water's edge sent shivers up his spine.

"Isn't this beautiful," Ava said, now holding him tightly around the waist.

"Yes, you are," he said, looking into her eyes.

"Let's sleep on the beach and watch the sun come up," Ava said. "That would be so beautiful and romantic."

"It'll be cold," Able said, as the voice of reason. "We can sleep inside and wake up early enough to see the sunrise. It will be much more comfortable."

"Please, please, please let's stay out here," Ava pleaded. "Let's just set up camp right here and stay warm with blankets and body heat."

There was a short pause, then she said with her best "puppy dog" look, "Please, honey bun, pleeaassee."

He really didn't need much convincing, so they headed back to the house for the necessary supplies. First, they had to get into the cottage and that meant breaking in through the infamous bedroom window. He prayed that one of his uncles hadn't gotten a wild hair and fixed the window lock since his last breaking and entering.

James gave him a leg up as he grabbed the edge of the porch roof and held on tight. He stepped on James' shoulder, then his head and clamored for another inch of roof. He was able to swing one leg up on the roof and James pushed his dangling foot up with both hands. Able was sure they looked like a couple of bumbling idiots. He finally dragged his other leg up on the roof and pulled his body up scraping along the asphalt shingles with each tug. He went to the far right window, popped out the bent screen, threw up the sash and toppled into the bedroom. There was usually a bed under the window, which made tumbling in much easier and pain free. One of his aunts must have rearranged the furniture, so he hit the hardwood floor with a thud. His aunts were always rearranging things in the cottage and moving pictures to different walls. One aunt would arrange things her way for her week, then another aunt would change it back the next week. It was a never ending merry-go-round of finding the perfect spot for beach-themed paintings and knick-knacks—an interior decorator's worst nightmare.

Able brushed himself off and went downstairs to let everyone in the front door. Ava and Able went straight to the linen closet and grabbed several blankets and pillows. James and Missy chose the creature comforts of the front bedroom and quickly closed the door behind them. Able heard them giggling loudly as they jumped into the old metal bed that squeaked loudly anytime you moved a muscle.

Ava and Able bedded down in a clearing where the boardwalk disappeared into the main strand. The sandy depression was surrounded by four small sand dunes covered with cattails and sea grass. The dunes were only about three feet high, but sheltered them from the cool wind that blew off the ocean. They stretched a blanket over the sand and pulled the other two blankets over them. They snuggled up close together under the moon and stars. It was very cozy and romantic . . . just like Ava said it would be.

The cattails danced in the wind as the waves crashed against the shore. There was the occasional cackle from sea gulls soaring overhead and the random "yee haw" and nonsensical blathering from drunk red necks stumbling home after a night of boozing it up. In the summertime,

Able's family would sometimes discover drunks sleeping at the end of their walkway and one time they discovered a guy who passed out in the hammock on their porch. It was a nice beach, mind you, but there were plenty of drunks to go around.

Ava looked into his eyes and smiled sweetly. She pushed the wind-blown hair out of his eyes and kissed him lightly on the lips. A surge of emotion ran through him from his head to his tippy toes. This was new territory for him and he really got caught up in the moment. They kissed and touched each other gently and lovingly. Their bodies became entangled as they rolled around on the blanket kissing with a passion that he did not know existed on this earth. The moon shined brightly and it lit up Ava's face in a hazy blue-gray sheen. Her blue eyes reflected the moonlight, which gave them a metallic glaze. He found himself staring deeply into her eyes, entranced by their connection. At that moment, he was convinced that everyone on earth has a soul mate and he knew that this girl was his. He vowed to himself to love her always–come hell or high water. So, he thought, this is what people mean when they say, "you'll know" when it's true love. It was that simple.

"Able," Ava said in a whisper. "I want to make love with you." She smiled and touched his face gently. "I love you, darling, and want to make love."

This request had never been made of him before and he was really caught a bit off guard. His heart pounded hard inside his chest. So hard, if fact, that he thought it would leap from his body and dance a jig right there in the sand. He looked into Ava's eyes. All of his fears and insecurities melted away in an instant. She made him feel so loved with just a simple look.

"I love you too, Ava," he said softly touching her cheek. "I didn't realize I could love someone this much, this soon, but I love you more than anything in the world." It was the first time he ever told a girl that he loved her—except for his old dog and he didn't think that really counted. He still missed that sweet puppy and she died ten years ago.

He began to slowly unbutton Ava's blouse, kissing each bit of flesh unveiled. She unbuttoned his shirt and this time left all the buttons intact. It wasn't the rushed, ripping off of clothes like in the movies, or the tug-of-war he usually encountered when trying to remove a girl's top. It was a methodical and patient process that took a good bit of time. Their intensity increased with the loss of each garment–remove shirt–kiss, slide off pants–kiss, pull off socks–kiss, unlatch bra–kiss, step out of underwear–kiss, and with the passing of every second a wave of emotion surged within each of them.

They lay naked in the sand with blankets pulled over them and clothes strewn about. They touched and kissed

each other as the love seemed to spill out of them without effort. They did not have much experience in the love making department, but it all seemed to come rather naturally and somewhat gracefully, believe it or not.

He hadn't thought about protection for their beach trip–the idea of him actually having sex with Ava never really crossed his mind before that very moment. He didn't think about how long he would last, or how good it would be, or what crazy position they would try, or how he would embellish the story when his buddies asked for details, or even the realization that he was going to make love for the first time ever . . . none of the usual male sex thoughts entered his brain.

The only thought he had was how much he loved this woman and how good she made him feel when he was with her. There was no official foreplay, not the kind of stuff you usually hear about, although the passionate kissing and hugging and touching for thirty minutes probably counted if they were keeping score. He rolled over and lay on top of her as they continued to kiss madly. Without even thinking about it he found his way inside her. She was warm and wet. They began to make love gently and quietly. They held each other close and touched and kissed, while their bodies moved slowly together. Their lovemaking seemed to use more of their hearts than the other essential body parts. Able was pretty sure that he had never given a girl an orgasm before—a real one anyway—but after several minutes both of their bodies shuddered with ecstasy in the night air. He rested on top of her with their bodies now completely still and held her tightly. He could feel her body throbbing beneath him and the pounding of her heart against his chest.

"I love you so much, Ava," he said.

Although it was a cool, early September night they were both wet with perspiration. He pulled the blankets over them and held her close . . . flesh pressing flesh. He kissed her lips, then buried his head in the nape of her neck and nuzzled her gently. He kissed her neck, then her lips, then her cheek.

"What's the matter, honey bun?" he asked, tasting a salty tear. They didn't really have any nick names yet, but he was always fond of "honey bun."

Ava sniffed and wiped her tears away with the back of her hand. "Nothing," she said at first with a strained voice and cried softly. Able lay there and looked at her with a puzzled expression on his face. He still hadn't figured out women, but this was one time when he was completely stumped.

"I, I don't know," she continued. "I've never felt that . . . that inten . . . that intensely before."

He knew that Ava was not a virgin . . . far from it, actually. That fact never bothered him, not really. So, it was surprising to Able that their lovemaking affected her so much. It made him feel good that he could evoke so much emotion from another person. They held on to each other tightly and professed their undying love for one another right there in the sand, witnessed only by the moon and stars. They curled up in the blankets and Ava fell asleep in his arms. He looked toward the sky, closed his eyes tightly and prayed to God that she would love him forever.

An hour later the sun peeked over the horizon and cast a yellow-orange hue across the morning sky. The ocean was calm and the waves rolled in and crashed neatly on the shore. Sea gulls cawed as they hovered behind shrimp boats looking for scraps. A flock of pelicans soared in formation just above the cresting waves. *This is why I love the beach*, Able thought.

He leaned over and kissed her cheek, salty-sweet. "Ava," he said quietly and gave her a gentle nudge. "Here's your sunrise."

Ava sat up and looked out at the view. Her eyes reflected the early morning light as she looked out over the lovely beach scene.

“Oh, it’s beautiful, darling,” she said. She breathed in deeply and her senses filled with the glory of an early fall morning along the Georgia coast. Then she turned to Able and their eyes met. She smiled a loving smile and asked, “Will you make love with me again, darling?”

Chapter Eleven

Ava rang the doorbell and waited for a minute. No one answered. She tested the front door and it opened with a loud click. She stuck her head in and called out. No response. The coast was clear.

She walked inside Able's parents' home in downtown Savannah and stood on the large Persian rug in the foyer. She admired the fine furnishings that seemed to be everywhere. Portraits hung on the walls with other expensive works of art, sculptures were placed strategically around the rooms for just the right look. *Nice,* she thought, *very nice.* Ava walked through the entire downstairs to get the lay of the land, then went to the second floor just out of curiosity. *Definitely professionally decorated,* Ava thought, *everything matches so well.* The master bedroom had a four-post bed with a beautiful canopy and gold bedding with matching throw pillow with black tassels. A Queen Anne style high boy

stood gracefully on one side of the room and a gold and red striped wing-back chair with ottoman on the other. The side tables and lamps on either side of the bed were fabulous. Nice, very nice.

After a short tour of the other bedrooms upstairs Ava went down to the library. She opened all the cabinets until she found the liquor. She picked up a half-empty bottle of bourbon and took a swig. She smacked her lips . . . not bad. She set the bottle back in the cabinet and pulled out another. It was a full fifth of Absolut vodka, her favorite. She broke the seal and put the bottle to her lips. *Glug, glug, glug.* The liquid ran down her throat easily and instantly made her feel warm all over. She could drink vodka all day long. She slid the bottle into her book bag and moved on to the dining room.

The center piece of the dining room was a beautiful chandelier made of glass crystals that hung just above the large mahogany dining table. The table could easily seat ten people, four on each side and two on either end. Ornate Chippendale chairs filled each space around the table and two lovely sterling silver candelabra stood on either side of the centerpiece–an arrangement of pussy willows in a tall glass vase. Simple, yet elegant.

A large hunt board was on one wall with a recently-polished coffee and tea silver service displayed on top. She slid open the top three drawers to find fine sterling silver flatware in one, sterling silver serving dishes in the middle drawer and small sterling silver serving bowls in the last. This is perfect, she thought. She gently loaded the necessary pieces into her book bag and tried not to bang them too much.

She continued on to a glass cupboard that displayed the fine china. She pulled out several large plates with a swirling gold and black design around the edge and a few matching platters. She opened a drawer on the built-in cabinet to find linen napkins and a linen table cloth that suited her taste just fine. Ava put all of these items in a brown grocery bag that she found under the kitchen sink. She stacked them carefully and placed a napkin between each plate and wrapped the other dishes in the table cloth. She wanted to make sure they got to their destination unharmed.

Ava went through the checklist in her mind. *Yes, got it, got it, got it . . . oh, one more thing,* she thought. She opened a door in the hallway between the dining room and the kitchen that went down to the basement. Ava flicked on the light and walked slowly down the steep stairs. She was right. The small, dark basement was a well-stocked wine cellar with all four walls covered floor to ceiling with dusty bottles from France, Spain, Italy and a few selections from California. Ava was no connoisseur, so she randomly selected several bottles of red that she thought would be tasty. Before she headed back upstairs she grabbed a bottle of Cote de Rhone champagne from an open case that sat in the corner.

Nice haul, she thought. *This should do just fine.*

Chapter Twelve

The fall dance at St. Margaret's was in late October and, of course, Ava forgot to tell Able about it until the last minute. Ava's mother actually had a dress made for the occasion and shipped it in from Charleston. Her mother was a very fancy Southern lady and wanted Ava to be fancy, too. Unfortunately for her mother, Ava was a bit wilder than her proper upbringing usually allowed. It was a beautiful dress, though, in pale yellow silk with white trim. It was form fitting and went down below her knees, so she had to walk in short ladylike steps or she would rip out the hem. It hugged her heart-shaped backside perfectly and had a low swooping neckline that showed plenty of cleavage. Ava had one of those hour glass figures, like women from the fifties, that really knocked Able off his feet. The dress looked fabulous on her, but Able couldn't wait to take it off.

The dance was one of those annual events that drove all the girls crazy, but in a good way. They spent time pick-

ing out their dresses and all of their accessories—boy, can girls accessorize. Each little social clique decided who would double or triple date with whom and where they would take their dates for dinner. And, most importantly all the girls had a few months of testing the waters at frat parties and clubs to determine which lucky boy would be chosen as their escort. Some girls took dates who they knew would be fun—at the dance and afterwards—but the type of boy they could toss aside like a used rag once the night was over. You know . . . fun and done. Then there were other girls who would bring their long-time boyfriends. Of course, some of the girls with serious boyfriends would most likely have the night end up in a fight over some stupid misunderstanding. Able had heard of fights that started up right out of the blue and ruined perfectly good dates.

"Peaches, I swear I wasn't staring at that girl's chest," the boyfriend would say, pleading for forgiveness. "She just walked in front of me and they just happened to be in my field of vision."

Poor sap. It happened every year at every dance around the world, Able was sure—and this dance would be no different. Someone would go home mad over a quick glance at some other girl's cleavage, or for not being told that she looked beautiful a million times. That kind of stuff just killed Able. It was almost as if some girls looked for reasons to get pissed off at their man–and it always seemed to be at a moment when they should be having the most fun, too. What a waste.

Actually, Able was excited about the dance. He was no Fred Astaire or anything, but he could dance pretty well—better than most guys his age, anyway. His mother made him take cotillion for a million years and some of that stuff really soaked in. He was also excited because this was the first time that Ava and he were going out in such a large group of people they both knew. He wasn't sure what you called it, but there was something about being seen out with a beautiful woman that made other guys jealous as hell. It had never happened to Able before, so he was looking forward to it. Ava was the kind of girl who evoked jealousy even from perfect strangers—girls and boys. That's how beautiful she was.

They were out at a bar a few weeks before, just sitting on some bar stools and minding their own business when this pretty boy, jock type walked right up to them.

"Hey, beautiful," he said. His chiseled jaw moved effortlessly and his white teeth sparkled. "Can I buy you a drink?"

Able leaned in towards him sheepishly. "No, thanks," he said and patted him on the shoulder. "I've got a drink right here buddy, but thanks."

He gave Able a "who the fuck are you" look, then slid over to block him out of the way. He put his hand on the bar between Able and Ava and turned his back to Able.

"What do you say, beautiful?" he tried again.

"I'm sorry," Ava said pushing the pretty boy aside as she stood up to put her arm around Able. "But this adorable man right here gives me everything I need and then some." She gave him a quick kiss and looked back at the guy, who was completely dumbfounded.

"You're kidding me, right?" said the pretty boy. He couldn't believe that he was being shot down in the first place, but being beaten out by the likes of a guy like Able was just too much for his simple mind to grasp.

"Orgasms every night and sweetness all day don't lie, baby." Ava said. She put her hand on Able's inner thigh, real close to you know what, and made a moaning sound as she rubbed against Able for full effect. "He's more than most women can handle," she said, then leaned in and gave Able a huge kiss just to piss off Pretty Boy even more.

"You could've had all this," said the pretty boy with his arms outstretched, then he tapped his chest. "Your loss, baby, your loss."

Pretty Boy walked away in disgust as Able sat there grinning ear to ear. Able waved goodbye just using his index finger to pile on the sarcasm. "Keep walking pencil dick," he yelled. Thankfully, Pretty Boy was too far away to hear him.

Ava was used to that type of attention, but Able couldn't believe that had actually happened. It happened several more times over the next year to his amazement. He realized that he was no stud bolt, but having guys approach his girlfriend when he was right there with her was a bit demoralizing. Ava always defended him, though, and knew just how to get him back up, emotionally speaking, of course. He didn't realize there were so many assholes out there. If that was the kind of shit that women put up with on a regular basis, Able thought, he wanted to apologize for his gender.

Chapter Thirteen

They were double dating to the dance with Missy and James—they were like four peas in a pod and had been hanging out a ton since early September. The girls planned an extra special evening for them, which they kept very secret. They told James and Able to meet them in the Rose Garden at eight o'clock sharp, dressed and ready to be amazed. That would give them plenty of time to eat and drink before getting to the dance around eleven. The Rose Garden was where they would go sometimes to drink, or get high. There was an outdoor theater with lots of nooks and crannies where young lovers could hide. The Rose Garden was behind the theater and was quite pretty with a million different types of roses. There were walking paths all through the garden with a fountain in the middle.

Able's parents were out of town on another business trip, so he had the house to himself. He looked sharp in his black houndstooth jacket, dark gray pants and wing tip shoes . . . perfect for cuttin' the rug. You really don't want any traction on the dance floor or you may break an ankle mid twist . . . a nice slick leather sole is best. He borrowed one of his stepfather's ties that he was sure cost about a million bucks. He never let Able wear any of his stuff when he was around, because he thought Able would ruin it.

"This is the highest quality material," he would say each time Able asked to borrow a shirt or tie or jacket. "When you learn how to take care of your own things, then I'll consider letting you borrow something of mine." Fat chance that would ever happen, so Able borrowed things when his stepfather was not around.

Able had some time before James came to pick him up, so he went downstairs and made himself a drink. He looked in his parents' liquor cabinet and pulled out a bottle of Old Grand Dad bourbon. He mixed about two fingers of bourbon with ginger ale and ice in a short, fat glass. The glass had a gold ring around the rim that made it look real fancy. He learned a good bit about mixing drinks at his parents' cocktail parties by playing waiter and just listening. He could tell who the neighborhood drunks were by how they ordered—three fingers of Scotch on the rocks was a sure sign of a drunk, not to mention the constant red nose with rosy cheeks. The standard bourbon and ginger or gin and tonic were ordered by the light social drinkers who would nurse one drink all night long, maybe two if they didn't live too far away.

He picked up his drink and swirled it around for a second, then drank it down fast. It burned as it ran down his throat and kind of took his breath away. It made him a bit flush and his body felt warm from head to toe. He made another drink and went to the living room to wait for James.

His parents' house was pretty fancy with antiques everywhere and portraits of dead ancestors on the walls. He was usually not supposed to go into the living room. It was only used for cocktail parties and other special occasions, but he considered this occasion to be special enough.

He was sitting there trying to remember his relation to the dead people hanging on the walls when James came busting in the front door. "Let the games begin!" he yelled loudly. "Brother Curran, our beautiful women await!" James was good at being overly dramatic. He always tried to make a grand entrance and usually did whether you wanted him to or not.

"Let me fix you a drink, old boy," Able said in a bad English accent.

"What are you having, brother Curran?" James asked in an accent that was even worse than Able's.

“A bit of Old Grand Dad with just a splash of ginger.”

“Sounds delightful,” James said. “Yes, please my good man, pour away.”

They sat down with their drinks and actually had a regular conversation with no accents, weird sounds or gestures for the first time in a long time. They wondered what the girls were up to and talked about their plan of coming back to Able’s parents’ house after the dance. He showed James what room he and Missy would stay in. They put a few condoms in the drawer of the night stand just in case. Able had done the same thing in his room since he was pretty sure he would get lucky. He laid out their best towels for everyone to use the next morning and put little decorative soaps on top of each towel to make it like a classy hotel. Earlier, he had gone to the store and bought orange juice and a dozen Krispy Kreme donuts for breakfast. Real classy, he knew but it wasn’t like he was going to make Eggs Benedict or anything.

James and Able sat in the living room, drank their bourbons and talked about the girls. It surprised Able, but none of the conversation was about sex. They both opened up and told each other about how deeply they cared for their girl and how they were different than anyone they ever dated.

“Do you think you’ll ever get married?” Able asked James.

"Probably . . . yeah, for sure," he said changing his mind mid-thought. "I think I'll marry Missy one of these days, you know, once I finish medical school and everything. She's perfect; perfect for me anyway. You?"

"Well, I want to get married," Able said taking a sip of his bourbon. "It has to be Ava, 'cause I don't think I'll ever love anyone else this much. I'm just afraid that I'm not good enough for her. We'll see."

"Hell, she's lucky to have you, man," said James raising his drink. "Here's to you being a fine bastard and one helluva catch, my friend."

They raised their glasses for an air clinky clink, then took a big swig.

Their conversation morphed into talking about their children playing together someday and they both hoped that the kids would get their mothers' good looks. It was kind of a weird conversation for two nineteen year old boys to have, but it happened just the same.

"If I have a little girl she'd better not look like me," said James taking a swig of bourbon. "She'll be in big trouble if she does—especially when she hits those teenage years. Can you imagine me as a girl? Man, I'd be so ugly even I wouldn't ask myself out." James shook his head to clear the thoughts of himself as a girl. "Well, at least she would have a nice jump shot," he added.

"I don't understand you, man," Able said, trying to sound disgusted at his shallowness. "That is so wrong—you've never had a nice jump shot. You've never had any game at all . . . you would be one butt ugly chick, though."

Able was in mid-laugh when James threw one of his mother's good pillows at him from across the living room. He put up his arm to block it, but it ricocheted off his hand and nailed him right in the face. Able spilled his drink all over his mother's antique Persian rug.

"Asshole," Able yelled. "That better not leave a stain or your ass is grass."

"See that," said James. "I got game . . . and don't you forget it."

James tossed back what was left of his drink, while Able used his cocktail napkin to sop up the spilled bourbon and ginger. They made one last check of the house to ensure a smooth transition from getting down on the dance floor to just getting down. Once they confirmed that all systems were a go, they made a roadie drink then headed off to the Rose Garden to meet the girls.

Chapter Fourteen

They parked in front of the outdoor theater where they had parked many times before for marathon make-out sessions with a variety of cooperative co-eds. The whole area was pretty dark with just one lamp post at the entrance. Their eyes adjusted to the dark night as they walked along the path that led to the rose garden and the spot where the girls told them to report.

They made their way along the trail until they saw lights in the distance about a hundred yards away. As they got closer they saw the flicker of candlelight that lit up a beautifully set table. There was a linen table cloth, linen napkins, sterling silver flatware, several bottles of red wine and a bottle of champagne on ice. Two sterling silver candelabra with long white candles sat at the center of the table. The candles had already burned down about a quarter of their length. There was a waterfall of wax hanging from the candelabra and splats of wax on the table cloth.

A note on the table read: "Welcome to our bodacious boys. Tonight will be an experience to remember . . . we promise. Open the champagne, pour four glasses and prepare yourselves for the unexpected."

James and Able looked at each other and smiled wide. They slapped at each other with excitement, then quickly settled down before someone saw them acting a fool. They did as they were told and poured four glasses, then waited there talking in hushed tones while sipping their champagne. A few minutes later they heard footsteps coming from behind a row of rose bushes. The girls suddenly appeared out of the dark. They both looked stunning all dolled-up for the occasion.

Ava looked like a movie star in her dress with a mink stole around her shoulders. The candles lit her up like klieg lights during a premiere and she walked in with all the grace of a Monroe, Mansfield or Gardner—her father named her well. She looked like she had time-traveled from 1955 the way her hair was done up big and swoopy, the style of her dress, the large fake diamond jewelry and long white gloves. Able liked it.

They all hugged and kissed hello. Able ran his hand down Ava's smooth silky dress from her back to her curvy hips, then gently patted her bum. He gave her a glass of champagne and they all toasted to the night ahead of them.

There were several small plates of appetizers, so they ate and drank and talked.

In no time the champagne bottle was empty, so Able opened up a bottle of red and poured everyone a glass. He raised his glass to propose another toast to the night and their hostesses.

"To the most beautiful women I know," Able began. "Who have certainly planned the most unique dinner of anyone attending tonight's dance and who have already given me an experience that I will not soon forget. You are both wonderful and I'm honored to be here. Che..."

"Who are you?" James interrupted. "My goddamn father?" He raised his glass and said, "A toast . . . to getting wasted!"

"To getting wasted!" the rest of them shouted. They clinked glasses, then gulped down their wine like they were Tequila shooters. James immediately refilled everyone's glass.

Able picked up his fork and looked at it closely. "You know," he said. "This silverware looks very familiar."

He looked at Ava and she had a sheepish grin on her face. "Well," Ava finally said. "It's actually your mother's sterling silver . . . and her candelabra . . . and her table cloth . . . . and . . ."

"What!" Able said as he jumped to his feet.

He must have had a look of pure horror on his face thinking of the punishment waiting for him when this was found out. Ava quickly tried to appease his fears.

"Don't worry, darlin'," she said. "I'll polish everything and take the table cloth to the dry cleaners—she'll never know—I promise." She took hold of his hand and placed it on her breast—a trick that Able had come to expect over the past few months when she wanted her way—it usually worked.

"Don't be mad, honey bunny, I'll . . . I'll make it up to you." She pushed out her chest and smiled her she-devil smile.

His parents rarely locked their house and he must have unconsciously mentioned that little nugget of information to Ava. She also knew that his parents left town this morning and that Able had to work most of the day. She simply let herself in the house and shopped for the dinner accessories that suited her taste—his mother's very best stuff, mind you. He knew what she had done was bad, really bad. He would never in a million years think of walking into her parents' house and taking anything—much less their fine silver. But, since he was feeling no pain from all the alcohol and staring down at a lovely set of D-cups, he let the issue slide. She was always pushing the envelope, which was part of her allure, but sometimes she pushed it a bit too far. This was one of those times.

"Okay, Ava," He said pointing his finger at her. "You PROMISE to put all this stuff back just like it was, because I am too young to die. My mother would absolutely kill me if she found out. You know, she loves this silver service crap."

Ava grabbed his hand with its finger still extended. She slowly slid his finger into her mouth. She sucked on it for a second before slowly sliding it back out, then she kissed the tip of his finger. "There," she said. "All better?"

"It'll be fine, man," said James from the other side of the table. "C'mon, let's continue the par-taayy!" He raised his hands in the air and made his famous "whoop, whoop" sound, while dancing a little jig.

Easy for him to say. It wasn't his ass on the line. Able tried his best to put it out of his mind and enjoy the night. They all sat down at the table with full glasses of wine and hors d'oeurvres arranged beautifully on his mother's finest sterling silver trays.

They finished off the miniature egg rolls, pea pods and some crunchy Chinese bread things. The first bottle of wine went quickly and Ava reached under the table and pulled out another. Able opened the bottle and topped off everyone's glass. Ava asked if they were ready for the main course, which they were. She stood up, placed her thumb and index finger in her month and let out a loud whistle. She waved to the darkness, then sat back down.

James and Able looked around to see what the hell was going on, but they saw nothing. A moment later a waiter walked out of the darkness carrying a large covered tray with one hand and a linen cloth draped over his other arm. He placed the tray at the center of the table and removed the top. Steam billowed out from under the lid and a terrific smell filled the air. Platters of beef broccoli, sweet and sour shrimp, moo goo gai pan and an array of noodles were revealed. Several bowls of steamed rice and a small cup of fortune cookies were nestled in the middle of the other dishes. What a feast!

The waiter disappeared into the night, backing away from the table with a low bow every two seconds. The girls served their plates with a sampling of each dish. They were all delicious. The four peas in a pod laughed and ate and told stories, then laughed some more. The wine continued to flow as another bottle was plucked from under the table. It was the most fabulous dinner date that Able and James ever had, but it was about to get better.

Ava and Missy gave each person a fortune cookie and told everyone to take turns opening theirs. James went first. He cracked the cookie so hard it crumbled into itty bitty, almost inedible pieces.

"Hey, hey!" he yelled after glancing at his fortune. He read it out loud . . .

"It says, 'you will get laid tonight.' These things are real, right?" he asked all excited looking at each person for reassurance. They all laughed at the look on his face. "Seriously," he said. "This has to happen, right? It's my fortune, right?"

Missy gave him a kiss on the cheek, told him to be a good boy and she would think about it.

Able unwrapped his cookie and snapped it in two. He read it, "'Double your pleasure, double your fun—fuck twins.'"

"I didn't know you had a twin sister," Able said looking at Ava.

"Maybe it's referring to my other twins." She palmed her breasts, one in each hand and smiled her she-devil smile.

"Point taken, point taken," Able said placing the fortune in his coat pocket for future reference. He turned and nearly buried his nose in Ava's cleavage and said, "Nice to meet you ladies."

Ava and Missy opened their fortune cookies. They just happened to be the same fortune, which Able thought was planned all along. Their fortune read . . . "You possess a magnetism that attracts others."

Able was pretty sure he knew what magnetism the fortune referred to—the pure power of woman, for sure. The girls had them tied around their pinky fingers—at least on this night—and the boys would have done just about anything they asked.

Just when they thought the night couldn't get any better the girls asked if they wanted dessert. Of course, they did. So they unveiled yet another covered silver tray from Able's mother's collection. Missy lifted up the cover to reveal a pyramid of brownies. Some had nuts and some didn't, but they all contained an extra ingredient.

Able had never had pot brownies before, but they seemed to be just as potent as if they had smoked a joint—maybe even more so. Of course, within no time they were all Chinese-eyed and completely baked out of their gourds. Able guessed China was the theme of the evening. The girls laughed more than ever at the slightest remark, no matter how absurd. Missy tried to pronounce the name on the wine bottle with no success, which killed everyone. James was transfixed by a candle and just stared at the flickering light. He was pathetic. Ava was Ava. She seemed to be the least affected of any of them and was her jovial, sex-crazed self. Every few minutes she would kiss Able's cheek, tongue his ear, or rub his crotch until Able nearly burst through the thin layer of wool.

At one point, Able was drawn to his watch and stared at it for several minutes. "Holy shit!" he yelled with a laugh. "It's 1:30 in the morning. We missed the whole fucking dance."

James looked away from the candle for the first time in thirty minutes. "Dance? What dance, man?" he said in perfect stoner cadence.

They all fell out laughing, except for James, who went back to staring at the candlelight. None of them really cared too much about missing the dance. They were having a great time and that was what mattered most. The only real problem was that Ava's mother insisted that they send her a photograph. At dances they make a stupid looking backdrop of hay and corn stalks or something like you're out on a farm. You have to listen to some bonehead photographer tell you to hold your head "like so." Those pictures never look very natural, but for some reason it's been going on for a million years with no end in sight.

Ava actually started to get upset, not from missing the dance, but at the prospect of not having a photograph to send her mother. Able told her that the next week they would make an appointment with a cheesy photographer and wear the same clothes. Her mother would never know the difference. That seemed to calm her down enough to forget about it for the time being. They actually did have a picture taken the next week and sent if off to Ava's mother. She thought they both looked "lovely."

They decided to head back to Able's parents' house since it was awfully late and there was nothing left to consume. Able took one candelabra to light their way down the path. The candles were now just flickering nubs of wax, but they still lit the way. Ava gathered up the four corners of the table cloth to make a satchel and all the dishes, platters and extra food slid down to the middle. She tied the four corners together and hoisted the makeshift sack over her shoulder. She looked like Mrs. Santa Claus in two inch heels. At the time, Able was too wasted to think about his mother's dishes and sterling silver getting beat all to hell.

Missy was the least drunk of anyone—at least she was the only one who could touch her nose during their impromptu sobriety test in the parking lot—so she drove them in James's car to Able's house. It was crazy to even think about driving, but they were stupid, horny teenagers.

They arrived in one piece—thank goodness. Each couple stumbled to their assigned bedroom, but of course, the elaborate sex plans disappeared the moment they climbed in bed. The only affection Ava and Able could muster was to nuzzle against each other before passing out in their Sunday best.

Able didn't even get a kiss goodnight, but he had a date that he would never forget.

Chapter Fifteen

St. Margaret's College: Savannah, Georgia

—February 1981—

Ava was campused on a regular basis for some offense or another.

They had to get creative in order to see each other. The magnolia tree as a meeting place was out of the question in the middle of winter. So, Ava would have Able sneak on campus and meet her at the gym, library or some other rather public place. When they met at any of these places they were usually naked in a matter of minutes–well, maybe just a little bit naked. They would talk, fool around and sometimes have sex if the coast was clear. If he heard a door open or commotion of some sort it would scare his clothes back on—although Ava never seemed to be affected by anything. She was always ready to do anything for fun and never seemed to get embarrassed, or fear anything at all. Able couldn't understand how she could so blatantly break the school rules and continually involve herself in socially unacceptable behavior. He did it sometimes too, but at least he felt bad about it.

One day they met at the school gym, one of their regular meeting places. It was one of those old gyms that doubled as the school theater with a stage at one end of the basketball court covered by a large royal blue curtain. They would hide behind the curtain among all the props from the latest play and just hang out for a while. On that day, Ava wanted to have sex in the middle of the basketball court, so, of course Able agreed. If you didn't know, nineteen year old boys are pretty much a walking erection and Able was no different. He was half naked with his pants around his ankles in mid-thrust when the basketball team filed in for their afternoon practice—all girls mind you. He pretty much mooned the entire team—and then some. He ran for the nearest exit pulling his pants up with one hand and carrying his shirt and coat with the other. Ava sat in the middle of the basketball court—legs spread with her underpants around one ankle—laughing at the top of her lungs. She was campused for a week.

Ava always liked to live on the edge, and she liked to push Able to the edge. One cold winter's day she convinced him to sneak up to her dorm room, which was totally against the rules. It was a difficult task since the Mole was constantly monitoring the hallways and there were several "Ms. Goodie-Two-Shoes" living in the dorm who would tattle in a second if given the chance. Ava recruited several of her hall mates to stand guard while a few other girls pretended to be in a cat fight at the other end of the building to create a distraction. Once Able snuck in the front door it was an all-out sprint up the stairs and down the hall to Ava's room.

By the time he got there she was already half naked—lying on the bed in a skimpy short night gown—Able thought it was called a teddy or chemise or something like that. His mind couldn't find the right word for the garment, but whatever it was Ava looked sexy as hell wearing it. The moment the door closed behind him she said, "Get over here and fuck me."

Ava had never used *that* word when referring to their love making and to tell you the truth, it kind of bothered him. Actually, she had been acting a bit strange over the past few weeks, enough so that he noticed a difference in her behavior. The loving, caring Ava was nowhere to be seen and a more selfish, uncaring side emerged. He wasn't quite sure what to do about it, but he got naked and jumped in bed just the same.

The sex was rougher than ever before and Ava seemed a little possessed by something. She was making strange noises and moaning much louder than usual—almost like she wanted to get caught. He had to admit that it made him a bit uncomfortable. He tried to get her to

quiet down. Of course, his "shushing" led to her screaming bloody murder—well, moaning at the top of her lungs, really. He tried to put his hand over her mouth when she got real loud, but she just pushed his hand away and was even louder on purpose. Then, all of the sudden, she began to laugh hysterically with this crazed look in her eye. Able freaked out slightly and stopped to try and calm her down.

"What are you doing?" Ava yelled. "Don't you dare stop fucking me!"

There was a hard knock on the door.

"What's going on in there!" It was the Mole. "Unlock the door this minute!"

"Holy shit," he whispered to Ava. "We're busted."

Now he was really freaking out. He jumped out of bed, grabbed his clothes and crawled into Ava's closet. He sat as far back as possible and didn't make a sound. Ava wasn't fazed at all. She got up slowly, put on her bath robe and opened the door. The Mole barged in looking around the room and under the bed.

"All right, who's in here with you, Ava?" the Mole asked.

"No one," answered Ava in a bitchy tone. "I'm all by myself."

"I'm tired of all this foolishness, Ava," she said. "Now tell them to come out here this minute."

Ava went to her bed side table and opened the drawer. She reached in and pulled out a purple vibrator with little nodules all over it. She recently purchased her new toy during a school trip to Washington, DC. Somehow she knew of a place called Pleasure Island that sold all kinds of kinky sex things. When she informed Able that she was going to buy a vibrator he told her to get a small one, but she didn't listen.

"Can't a girl have a little fun by herself without being accused of something every time she makes a noise?" said Ava waving the vibrator in the air. "Or do you hate fake dicks, too?"

"How dare you! Put that thing away!" the Mole said furiously. "I know someone is in here," she yelled at the walls. "Come out this instant or I will call the police!"

Able panicked. He hadn't been in trouble with the cops since the Halloween egging incident of 1973 and he didn't need that kind of trouble again. The Mole called out again and said it was her last warning. Able believed her. Without thinking too carefully, he burst out of the closet yelling like a madman. He ran across the room bare-assed nearly knocking the Mole over. There were girls lining the hallway listening to the commotion and he ran past all of them holding his clothes in both arms with no way to cover up. He flipped and flopped as he ran down the hallway, through the emergency exit and down the stairwell, then out the front of the building.

He ran across the edge of campus to his car down the street—buck naked the whole way. He put his hand on the dashboard and said a quick little prayer. Thankfully, his shit-box of a car started on the first try. *Thank you, God,* he thought. He drove home naked with a pile of clothes in the passenger seat.

Ava called later that evening to apologize for the way she acted. Of course, he told her it wasn't a big deal and that he still loved her. It was better that she heard that rather than get an ear full from him, too. She was nearly expelled from school this time, but her parents swooped in to save the day. He was not sure what they did, but part of the deal was that Ava had to see a psychiatrist for a few months. She was fine with this arrangement and twice a week for the next two months she just told the shrink what he wanted to hear. In the end, he gave her a glowing report with the only negative being that she craved attention. No shit, Sherlock.

Parents always seem to think that saving the day is a good thing, but really it just postpones the inevitable. Sometimes, they should just let their kids crash and burn, so they learn their lesson the hard way. Parents can be the biggest enablers of them all when they're acting out of love and kindness, but that usually just makes things worse.

Chapter Sixteen

Ava pulled her forest green Audi convertible into the parking lot of a large brick office building a few blocks from downtown. She opened her glove compartment and pulled out a pint of vodka. Without even looking to see if the coast was clear, she tipped the bottle up and downed half the pint with a few big chugs.

Then, she pulled out a bottle of Listerine and took a swig. She swished it around in her mouth for a full minute. Her mouth began to burn and her eyes watered. She opened the car door and spat liquid foam all over the asphalt. She looked in the mirror—no adjustments were necessary.

Dr. Frank Thomas had a modest little office and shared a receptionist with the other offices on the third floor. Thelma Green, the receptionist, always studied Dr. Thomas' patients when they checked in, since he was the only psychiatrist on the floor. She wondered what was wrong with each patient and made up little scenarios to entertain herself on slow days. Ava sat in the waiting area on an old, red leather sofa with cracks all over it. This really needs recovering, she thought. She picked up *Psychology Today* off the cheap, flea market coffee table and flipped through the pages just to kill time. Thelma was sure that Ava was getting the help necessary to deal with her parents' nasty divorce. Poor child. She played out a quick little scenario in her head of Ava's father cheating on his mother with his secretary and beating the children.

After a few minutes, there was a high-pitched *ding* from behind the reception desk. "You can go on in now, sugar," said Thelma Green in a caring tone. "The doctor's ready for you."

Ava opened the door and sauntered over toward the doctor's desk. The doctor's back was turned as he searched a filing cabinet for her records. She unbuttoned the third button from the top on her blouse and pushed her bosoms together while she had the chance. She sat in the chair directly across from the desk and crossed her legs. Her long, black skirt was split up to mid-thigh, so plenty of skin showed if she wanted it to—and she did. She leaned forward slightly and pushed her bosom together with her arms as she rested her hands on her bare knee.

"Ms. Dubose, I presume," said the doctor as he pulled the file off the shelf and turned around slowly to face Ava. "So, how are we doing today?"

When he saw Ava staring back at him he froze for a moment. Then, he tossed the file on the desk, took off his bi-focals, ran his hand through his thinning hair and straightened his jacket. He scanned his new client quickly, but completely. She could tell that he was a bit stunned by the view. He wanted to make a good impression, even though Ava was a good twenty years his junior.

"Hello, Dr. Thomas," said Ava with a smile. "It's nice to meet you." She leaned over and shook his hand, then settled back in her chair—legs crossed and chest out. Ava learned the art of seduction early on and used it to her advantage whenever necessary.

The session was supposed to last for a full hour, but Ava started her getaway almost immediately, since Dr. Thomas looked to be such an easy mark. She talked about her feelings and how she was always the center of attention whether she liked it or not because of how she looked. The doctor nodded and every few minutes said, "um hmmm," to show he was paying attention. He rarely took his eyes off her and struggled to think of another question when Ava finished answering the last one.

Ava saw her opportunity in the doctor's eyes. She looked hard at the doctor and started to cry. She had always been able to make herself cry on cue, which got her anything she wanted as a child. It worked as an adult, too.

"I'm sorry," she said. "I just don't know what's wrong with me. I get so out of control sometimes for no apparent reason." She sniffled and took a tissue when the doctor held out a box of Kleenex. "Isn't there anything you can give me to settle my nerves?"

Ava cast the bait out there knowing full-well he would bite. They always did. Dr. Thomas pulled out his prescription pad and began to write and talk at the same time.

"Here's a little Valium that should make you less anxious," he said finishing his scribble. "Just take one when you need it, bedtime is best; and don't drink any alcohol with it, okay?"

"Oh, of course not," said Ava dabbing her nose and cheeks. "I really don't drink that much anyway."

"Good, good," said the doctor handing over the prescription. "It's a bad habit to get into, especially for a pretty young girl like you."

Ava stood up and thanked the doctor. He walked her to the back door where all of his patients exited, so they could keep a low profile.

"I'll see you again in a few weeks," he said. "That prescription should hold you until then."

"Thank you so much, Frank, ah, Dr. Thomas," she said. "See you soon."

Dr. Thomas opened the door and said goodbye. He stood at the door and admired Ava as she sashayed down the hallway. She knew he was watching and worked her walk for the full effect. Ava's walk was the equivalent to a snake charmer's instrument and evoked similar results . . . stunned obedience. She turned the corner at the end of the hall, paused to wave to the doctor, then was gone.

Chapter Seventeen

St. Simons Island, Georgia

—June 1981—

Summer was the first time that Ava and Able had been apart for any real length of time. She had gone home for Christmas and Easter break, but she came back to him pretty quickly. When she was away they talked on the phone every night for hours and hours, which drove their parents up the wall, he was sure.

This time, though, she would be gone for months on end staying at her family's vacation house near Charleston and working some crappy summer job. She told Able about the vacation house on John's Island and went on and on about how beautiful and natural it was there. It sounded a lot like his grandmother's cottage, but at a beach that hadn't been ravaged by developers yet. Developers were the worst. They were the only people Able knew who could look at a beautiful, natural setting and envision condos as far as the eye could see.

"Darlin', you must come up to John's Island for a weekend," Ava said during their first phone call of the summer. "It's just so beautiful here, plus, I know some great places where we can do it." Ava had become more of a horn-dog than Able, if that was even possible.

They wouldn't talk again for almost a month. Able called Ava each week on the day and time that they agreed to talk, but she was never around. Her mother would say that she was working, or out on the beach with her little sister or that she "hadn't seen her all day." She returned a few of his calls, but she always called when Able was at work or in class. He would save her messages on his answering machine and play them over and over again just to hear her sweet voice.

Able signed up for both sessions of summer school to try and make up for lost time. His being in school kept them five hours apart by car—six hours if you drove his piece of shit. Not seeing her just killed him. It really did. He was like a zombie, moping around campus and doodling her name in his notebook during class. He survived on reading old letters and surrounding himself with photographs of her, but it just wasn't the same as having her in his arms.

There was a one week break between summer sessions in mid-June. What he really wanted was to be with Ava, but he was forced to go to the beach with his family instead. He invited Ava to join them and was counting the seconds until her visit. She planned to drive up on Thursday for a long weekend. Able was about to bust waiting to see her again. Sure, he thought about the sex part, but he really just wanted to be with her—to touch her and smell her again. Man, was he whipped. Whipped like a dang mule, as his cousin John would say.

It was Thursday morning and Ava was to arrive that afternoon. He couldn't wait and was a nervous wreck for some reason. The phone rang and after a few minutes his mother called out for him. He ran down to the kitchen and picked up the receiver.

"Hey, it's me," said Ava, rather matter-of-factly.

"Hey, honey bun," Able said smiling. "I can't wait to see you this afternoon."

"Well," Ava said in a tone that screamed bad news. "A friend of mine in Atlanta is really sick and she needs me to visit this weekend. Her father agreed to fly me down, so I'm leaving in just a little while. I'm sorry, but there's nothing I can do."

I know what you can do, Able thought, *tell your friend to take two aspirin and call a fucking doctor.* Rather than expressing his inner voice's suggestion, though, he did his best impression of a boyfriend who was understanding and supportive. This friend better be on her death bed. If his weekend rendezvous was being ruined by a simple head cold, he would scream.

Ava apologized again and said that they would see each other soon, so not to worry.

It had been over a month since they last saw each other and Able could hardly stand it any longer. The few times they did speak on the phone were not like the times before—Ava sounded distant. She wasn't gushing with love like before and she would giggle during non-giggle moments—like when Able told her his old dog died. She said she was sorry, but then let out a loud laugh. It gave him a weird feeling; you just don't laugh when someone tells you their dog died—you just don't.

He told her to call him when she got back from Atlanta to give him a medical update—he was curious about her deathly-ill friend.

"Ok," she said. "I'll call you the second I get home—promise."

"All right, honey bun, I'll be thinking of you." Able said.

He made little smooching noises before he hung up, which was their usual routine. Ava didn't reciprocate the air smooch and it bothered him.

He sat there for a minute and thought about the past month—the missed phone calls, the weird behavior, the emotional distance he was feeling from Ava. He could sense that she was drifting away, but he didn't know quite how to bring her back. He figured that physical distance sometimes creates emotional distance and he wanted to close the emotional gap as soon as possible.

Chapter Eighteen

John's Island, South Carolina

—June 1981—

George Hunt took the mirror off the wall in the large living room of his family's plantation house and placed it carefully on the antique coffee table.

He poured powder from a small baggie onto the mirror, tapping the bag to get out every fleck. He chopped it up and spread it out, then he divided the powder into four equal lines. He removed his wallet from the back pocket of his well-worn jeans and pulled out a crisp $100 bill. He rolled the bill tightly and handed it to Ava.

"Ladies first," he said, and laughed loudly. "Even fucked-up I'm a Southern gentleman, huh, baby?"

Ava took the rolled bill and got down on her knees. Empty whisky bottles and pizza boxes littered the floor around her. She leaned over the mirror, held her left nostril closed with her index finger and sucked a line of powder into her right nostril. She dropped the bill and snorted continuously for several seconds. She grabbed at her nose and wiped at it madly to stop the burn.

"Good shit, huh, baby?" said George all excited. He grabbed the bill off the table, tightened it a bit, then snorted his line. "Fuck me! That's good shit!" He said, jumping around the table and wiping at his nose. "Whoa, hell yeah, damn good shit!"

George handed Ava the bill for her next line as he continued to bounce around the room, whooping every few seconds. She leaned down over the mirror again and caught her reflection. Her eyes were dark and gaunt. Her skin was pale. Her hair was greasy and unkempt. She sat up straight for a moment and thought about stopping, but she couldn't. She covered her right nostril this time and put the bill to her left side as she leaned down to the mirror again.

She snorted half the line.

"Damn it!" she yelled and threw the bill on the floor. She stood up and walked across the room out the French doors that opened onto a covered porch. She looked out over the salt marsh as the sun began to creep up the horizon showing just a hint of yellow haze. She remembered watching the sunrise with Able their first time making love on the beach. She was lost in the memory for a moment and smiled. Then, Ava covered her face with her hands and wondered when things turned so bad.

"Hey, baby," said a shirtless George as he joined her on the porch. "What's the matter? I've got more coke if that's what you're worried about—as much as you want, baby." He laughed a creepy, druggy-type of laugh and rubbed his flat, hairy belly.

"No, that's not it," said Ava staring out to the horizon. "I should really be getting home. The sun is starting to come up."

"Aw, come on, baby," said George, moving wildly around the porch, swinging his arms and wiping his nose every few seconds. "It's still early and I'm sure not ready to sleep. Hey, let's fuck some more. Want to fuck some more, baby?"

Ava turned and looked at George, who could not stay in one spot for more than a milli-second. He was handsome—well, usually—with curly brown hair and dark brown eyes. He looked like a life guard with his tanned, toned pecks and tight stomach. He'd been living off cocaine and pizza since his parents died three years ago. That was how he stayed so thin. He was the sole heir to their fortune and was happy to send his inheritance right

up his perfectly-proportioned Roman nose. He loved the old plantation more than anything else his parents left him. It was five hundred acres along the sound and salt marsh just north of John's Island. The house was full of expensive antiques, but a lot had been stolen, or broken, during George's week-long parties with friends over the years. George inherited the house in Charleston too, but he sold it a year after his parents died. It was from the early 1800s with a view of the Battery and was furnished with the finest antiques one could find. He sold it for fifteen million, fully furnished. The furniture alone was probably worth that much, but he didn't care. George bought a row house in the heart of old downtown Charleston on Broad Street near the shops and trendy restaurants. He mainly stayed there in the winter months and entertained those friends who liked him for all the wrong reasons.

He inherited his father's shipping business too, which was started by his great, great grandfather. The company executives of Palmetto Shipping International, who now ran the business, offered George a position as Vice President years ago, but George had no interest in working, since he made a million dollars a year for lying in the sun, lifting weights and doing blow all night long. His parents didn't seem to care about what he did when they were alive, so he figured, why should he care now that they're dead.

All told, he was worth about a hundred million.

Girls were never a problem for George. If his looks didn't get them, then his money did. Plenty of women had tried to hook him, but he'd have none of them—not long term anyway. He had gotten a vasectomy years ago to avoid any palimony suits, although his suitors didn't have a clue. One girl tried to trap him and took him to court to prove she was carrying his child. She thought she was in high cotton until George produced his medical records and the case was dismissed immediately. Not surprisingly, the girl had a miscarriage a few weeks later.

Ava met George when she was sixteen and staying with her Grande for the summer at the family cottage on John's Island. Her parents were traveling around Europe and didn't want to be weighed down by children. It only took a few weeks before she lost her virginity to him. It happened in the boathouse on the creek that snakes through the salt marsh behind the plantation house. They did it on top of a bunch of life preservers and blow-up rafts. The first time lasted all of thirty seconds, but they had all summer to practice. And they did.

Ava and George had hooked up almost every summer since then and had always talked about running away together. They got each other to start drinking that first summer, real drinking, although Ava had been nipping from her parents' liquor cabinet since she was twelve.

They experimented with drugs together and both developed addictions together. A match made in hell, right? One night during a cocaine-induced all-nighter, they planned to move to Los Angeles together and become famous.

Famous for what they didn't know just yet.

Chapter Nineteen

St. Simons Island, Georgia

—June 1981—

Able had planned to leave the beach cottage early Sunday morning to get back in time to prepare for the second summer session that started on Monday. It was only Saturday though, and he was about to jump out of his skin worrying about Ava. At breakfast, he told his parents that he really wanted to get a jumpstart on school, which was a pile of you-know-what, so he needed to go ahead and hit the road. They were proud of his dedication to the books and all—there was that blind trust again. They kissed him goodbye and his mom handed him a bag of sandwiches as he walked out the door.

Of course, instead of heading west back towards school he went north towards John's Island, South Carolina.

John's Island was a good three hours away from Able's family's beach house. He had to travel on an old crappy two-lane highway most of the way. He got behind a couple of old farts in a Cadillac Seville with Florida license plates who drove slow as molasses. His little shit-box of a car didn't have enough horses to pass them when the opportunity presented itself. So, he drove ten miles under the speed limit until he reached a semblance of civilization where the highway grew to four lanes for a time. He zipped past the blue hairs in the right lane since they never moved over into the slow lane. There should be laws against really, really old people driving—they can be dangerous. Even though his car was a piece of crap it got like a million miles to the gallon, so he only had to stop a few times to fill up, grab a drink and take a leak. He was cruising down a stretch of highway just south of Charleston where a bunch of shanties line the highway. They were little stores where locals sold hand-woven straw baskets and knick-knacks. He pulled over at one of the many shanties to check it out and to pick out a present for Ava. There was an old black lady sitting in a rocking chair behind a table stacked with baskets and straw hats and things. She was working that rocking chair like crazy. She just sat there rocking and weaving, and weaving and rocking like she was on a mission or something.

"How you doing today, baby boy?" she said in an accent Able couldn't quite place. "The Lord done brought us another beautiful day, ain't He?"

“He sure has,” Able said looking up at the pale blue sky and squinting at the bright summer sun. “The Lord sure knows what He’s doing.” Able was trying to be deep, but he didn’t think it came across that way.

He smiled at her and she smiled back. When she smiled, her whole face curled up with a million wrinkles on her cheeks, forehead and around her eyes. She must have been about a hundred years old. Her fingers moved effortlessly as she weaved the basket she held in her lap and barked out prices for the items on the table without Able asking.

“Did you make all these things?” he asked.

“Me and my babies make it,” she said nodding to the other shanties nearby. “My babies and grand babies been he’pin since they could walk. I learn’t from my mama, they learn’t from me and the Lord keeps this old world turning.” She laughed loud and slapped at her knee. Her smile flashed large white teeth that stood out against her coal dark skin.

She stopped weaving and looked at Able closely. He was leaning on the table just looking at stuff. She rocked forward and reached out to touch his hand. Her old eyes twinkled when she smiled at him. She patted his hand gently, then held his hand in hers for a moment. Her long, rough, dark fingers cradled his small pale hand.

"It'll be all right, baby boy," she said squeezing his hand tightly and shaking it.

"What will be all right?" he asked, looking at her a bit puzzled and holding her hand.

"Everything, baby boy. Everything be all right," she said, as she looked at him with caring eyes.

"Ok, ah, thanks," Able said, not really knowing what to say.

"Baby boy," she said reaching into her apron pouch. "I want you to have this."

She leaned forward in her rocker and handed him a simple cross carved out of petrified driftwood. It was about two inches high, charcoal gray in color and rubbed smooth on all sides. A thick piece of leather was threaded through a hole in the top of the cross and knotted on the ends.

"How much?" he asked.

"Nothin', baby boy, not one red cent," she said. "That's from me to you." She placed her hand over her heart, then stretched her hand out towards Able as she spoke. She smiled her caring smile.

"You hold that tight when trouble come along, baby boy, and know the Lord will light your way."

"Thank you," Able said a bit stunned. "Thank you very much."

"You follow the Lord, baby boy," she said. "That's all the thanks I needs."

He bought a small woven basket for Ava and a Huck Finn looking straw hat for himself. He thanked the old woman again for the cross and walked toward the car.

"Ask the Lord to light your way, baby boy!" she called from her rocker. "Praise Jesus!"

Able turned to wave goodbye to the old woman, but she was back to her weaving and rocking. He held the cross she had given him in the palm of his hand and admired it for a moment. He squeezed it tightly and, for some reason, it gave him a sense of security. He pulled the leather necklace over his head and wiggled it left, then right to get it past his ears. The cross settled just below the nape of his neck and just above the large freckle on his chest. He turned the key several times and Millie started on the third try.

The road to John's Island was lined with two-hundred-year-old Live Oaks, Cypress and Pine. Spanish moss dripped from the tree limbs like syrup off a stack of hot cakes. The trees and tall marsh grasses swayed in the salty breeze. The two-lane road meandered for miles and miles through woods, then across marshlands, then through woods again. Able crossed several small bridges that leap-frogged from dry land to dry land and passed roads with names like Soggy Bottom and Free Man's Way. The marsh grass was spectacular in shades from bright green to honey gold and stretched for miles in some places. Small streams cut through the grass at low tide going this way and that created the perfect hiding place for many little creatures, Able was sure. A large Snowy Egret stood in knee deep water, biding his time for the right moment. In the blink of an eye he dunked his head under water and snatched up an unsuspecting fish innocently swimming by. A Great Blue Heron soared overhead, then skimmed the water to snatch up his lunch. He returned skyward and settled high up in a Palmetto to dine.

Able rolled down his window and the salt marsh air rushed in, hot and musty. Almost immediately beads of sweat formed on his brow. Sweat trickled down his face and neck, then soaked into the collar of his shirt. He crossed a long, steel bridge that spanned a large body of water and miles of salt marsh. Long docks stretched out across the marsh to boat slips on the water. Boats of every size and style were docked at the edge of the marsh or moored in deeper water. Ava was right—it was a beautiful place.

He finally arrived at the main road—the only road really—which was two lanes that ran parallel to the ocean. He could only turn to the right since there were mounds of soft sand to the left at the beach access. He turned right and drove slowly to take in all the sights, sounds and smells. There were old cottages on larger-than-usual lots along the ocean front and just a few houses on the other side of the street. Most of the cottages were made of cedar shake shingles and looked about a hundred years old. Others were sided with regular clapboard and just as old, but they were freshly painted in bright colors—canary yellow, sky blue and conch shell pink. Each cottage had a name carved in wood and displayed for all to see on the back of each cottage—The Great Escape, Columbia, SC; Sawyer's Solitude, Buford, GA; His Palmetto Pleasure, Greenville, SC; to name a few. Able continued down the main street for about a mile. He was looking for Ava's house, which was supposedly a huge, old shingled cottage that was dark gray—the color of naturally aged cedar—with white trim and a large white wrap-around porch. The sign on her cottage was: Gray Admiral, Sumter, SC, but he didn't see it yet.

Since most of the houses were on the ocean side, he kept looking to the left and didn't really look to the right side of the street. Then, something caught his attention and he quickly looked to the right. He passed a jogger running along the shoulder of the road. He adjusted his rear view mirror to get a better look as he passed by. The form was familiar and something made him pull over and stop. The jogger slowed down and stopped just behind his car. He turned around in time to see her take off her baseball cap as locks of blonde hair came tumbling down from underneath. It was Ava. He got out of the car and walked towards her. She breathed heavily and was sweaty in the afternoon heat of late June.

"Hey, honey bun!" Able said very excited. "What happened to Atlanta?"

He walked toward her for his first hug in a month, but she just pushed him away.

"What are you doing here?" she asked in frustration. "You're not supposed to be here!"

"What's the matter, honey?" he asked, confused. He reached out for her, but she backed away.

"Why are you here?" she cried out. "You're not supposed to be here!"

"I, I was tired of hanging out at our cottage," he stammered, a little freaked out at her reaction to seeing him. "So, I, I thought I'd come down here to see what you've been going on and on about." He reached out to touch her again and she pulled away again.

"What happened to Atlanta?" he asked. "You're supposed to be in Atlanta."

"No, no, no," she started to cry. "I thought we could get away without ever seeing you again. I thought that would be best . . . for both of us. I was trying to make it easier for you."

She cried louder and rambled on and on. Able didn't know what to do. "'We' who?" he asked. "You said 'we could get away', who is 'we'?"

"God dammit!" she buried her face in her hands and stood there shaking her head for a moment before she looked back at Able. "I've been seeing my old boyfriend for the past month," she said. "His family has a house down here and it just happened. We were partying one night and it just happened."

"What happened?" Able said. "You hooked up? That's okay, we all make mistakes, honey bun. I can forgive you for hooking up with an old boyfriend."

"You are such a goodie-two-shoes, Able—the good son!" she yelled. "I'm fucking him, okay, I've fucked him every day for the past month." She was hysterical and moving quickly from side to side as she spoke. She pushed his arm away every time he reached out for her.

She buried her face in her hands again and cried so hard her shoulders heaved. He was finally able to put his arm around her without being pushed away. It was the first time in a month that he was able to touch her. She sank into his arms and sobbed uncontrollably. He knew he should have been furious, but his only reaction was to comfort her. She cried and cried while he held onto her without shedding a single tear.

"We can get through this, honey bun," he said. "I still love you. We can get through this—I promise."

Ava looked up at him with those beautiful blue eyes with just a hint of bloodshot-red from crying like crazy. He held her face in his hands and wiped the tears from her cheeks. He leaned in and kissed her, a pure lip to lip kiss on the mouth. He felt the same jolt that he did the first time they kissed back at the fraternity house almost a year ago. He looked deep into her eyes and smiled.

"We'll get through this, honey bun," he said still holding her face in his hands.

Ava looked at him tenderly for just a moment, then the scowl suddenly reappeared on her face.

"Don't call me that!" she yelled. She knocked his hands away and took a step back. "No, we won't get through this," said Ava as she pushed him away. She wiped her tears and began to speak in a very matter-of-fact tone. "Look Able, I'm moving to Los Angeles with George. It's all arranged. We leave tomorrow and I'm not coming back to this God-forsaken place."

Able looked at her in sheer disbelief. He asked her what she was talking about—to explain this to him—but she just pushed him away and walked off. He ran after her and pleaded for her to stay with him. She kept walking and ignored him completely. Able grabbed her by the shoulders and stopped her. He held on tight and begged her not to go.

She stood still for a moment and stared at him with blank, uncaring eyes. "You're fucking pathetic," she said and pushed him away.

"Ava!" he yelled. He held onto her as she struggled to get away. "What are you doing? What's going on? I know you love me!"

"Get it through your fucking head, Able," she said with an anger that he had never seen in her before. "I love George. I've always loved George! You were just a play thing!" She quickly yanked her arm away from his grip and walked off. "Don't follow me, don't call me," she yelled without looking back. "I never want to see you again—never!"

Able stood there and watched her walk away. He was too stunned to cry–too stunned to feel anything really. He watched her for so long she got smaller and smaller against the horizon, eventually disappearing from view. He stood at the edge of the road and just looked to the last place he saw her—a few cars passed by within a foot of him and beeped, but he didn't even flinch. The sun

started to creep down in the western sky and it cast long shadows across the marsh and road. Finally, he turned and walked back to the car.

The old shit-box started on the second try. He made a U-turn and drove back down the beach road past The Great Escape, Sawyer's Solitude and His Palmetto Pleasure. He drove back from where he came . . . down the lonely two lane road toward the interstate and further away from his one true love.

The setting sun lit up the marsh with an orange-yellow hue that made the drive even more beautiful than it was earlier in the day. The marsh was more active now with jumping fish and a variety of seabirds in search of dinner. A Brown Pelican hovered high overhead before plunging into a school of bait fish like a missile.

Able pulled off to the side of the road at a small clearing that looked out over a large expanse of salt marsh. He just sat there and stared out into space as the magnitude of losing Ava began to well up inside him.

He thought back to the old black lady weaving baskets on the side of the road.

"Everything be all right, baby boy," she had said.

He wondered for a moment if she saw this coming, if she could see into the future. If anyone could see the future it would be her—she had that special look in her eye. How else could he explain her words?

His shoulders began to shake. His bottom lip began to quiver. A wave of emotion flooded his senses and tears began to stream down his face. He hugged the steering wheel and sobbed uncontrollably.

His whole body began to tremble. He gasped to breathe as wave after wave of emotion crashed down over him. He fell back against the old bucket seat and shook the steering wheel with all his might until it nearly snapped off in his hands. Tears streamed down his face. He had never experienced that level of sadness in his entire life. What was it about this girl that created such uncontrollable emotion? He climbed out of the car and walked to the edge of the marsh. The setting sun beat down on him in the lingering heat of the day.

"No, God, no," he wailed. He grabbed at his heart to keep it from shattering into a million pieces.

The cross the old lady had given him dangled from his neck. He pulled it over his head and held it up with both hands. He tried to focus on the cross through hazy, tear-soaked eyes. He didn't know how to handle losing Ava–or if he could handle it, really. His friends and family wouldn't understand the depth of his heartache. Even though they were young, this was more than puppy love

. . . much more. They would be supportive, of course, and try to convince him that "it's for the best," but he knew better. He knew that this was a special love—a soul mate—never to be duplicated.

The salty tears burned his eyes as they continued to flow freely down his face. He dropped to his knees and held the cross tightly in his hands out in front of him. The cross was silhouetted against the setting sun. All the colors of the sun seemed to jump out from every edge of the cross.

He remembered the basket weaver with her kind smile and caring touch. She seemed to be all-knowing and at peace in her world. His world was crumbling all around him and he didn't know how to stop it. He tried to focus on the cross again through tear-soaked eyes. He squeezed it even tighter than before. He didn't know what else to do.

"Please, Lord," he prayed. "Please, Lord, light my way."

Chapter Twenty

Los Angeles, California

—November 1982—

The room was loud with chatter as wanna-be stars practiced lines and waited their turn to audition for some stupid grocery store commercial. It wasn't the greatest gig in the world—it was a little on the cheesy side, really—but at least it paid pretty well for a day's work.

A woman handed out one-page scripts to everyone and then five minutes later began calling them in one by one. Able was trying out for the part of the farm boy who was supposed to be collecting eggs in the wee hours of the morning on the family farm. His line was, "Farm fresh goodness from our home to your table." He read his line out loud in a low whisper and thought about how to express himself as a farm boy.

"Farm freessh guutness from our hom to yer table," He read it with a strong country boy accent. *That sucked*, he

thought. He tried it several different ways and tried to capture just the right amount of country twang.

"Able Curran!" the woman behind the desk called out. "You're up!"

His heart jumped. His fellow wanna-be's watched as he made his way toward the door. He was pretty sure none of them wished him luck.

He walked into a small room with at least eight people staring at him—the director, the producer, some advertising agency suits and a handful of peons all holding clipboards. Everyone looked very chic with interesting glasses and stylish clothes—even the peons looked swanky. He walked over to the most important looking person in the room and handed her his resume with his headshot on the back of it.

His resume barely filled up half a page. It had the standard information on it, all his high school stuff: the athletic teams he played on, editor for the student newspaper, student government representative and the year he graduated. Some people, mainly the brainy variety, list their class rank; however, since he was like number fifty-five in a class of sixty, it wasn't impressive enough to put in black and white. Then he listed some general work experience from summer jobs with titles like "maintenance coordinator" for when he cut grass and "sales representative" for

Nice Ice, which was really just a snow cone cart on the boardwalk at the beach. Below that, he listed the plays he had acted in clear back to the Myrtlewood Elementary production of *Hansel and Gretel* in second grade. He played Hansel to some critical acclaim by the seven and eight year olds who attended the performance.

It was a pretty pathetic display of accomplishments over his twenty-two years on this earth, to tell you the truth. *You have to start somewhere,* he thought, and that was the best he could do.

He decided on his natural Southern accent for the audition. He grew up in the city, so he kind of had a city-Southern accent, which is nothing like what you usually hear on television. Actors usually butcher a Southern accent and make all Southerners seem like a bunch of backwoods idiots who still use a privy. That's an out house to the Yankees who don't know any better. There were certain words that sounded very Southern when Able talked, but most were just a bit softer and more rounded off than most folks. He sounded more like someone from *Andy Griffith* rather than *Dukes of Hazard.*

"Ok, Able," said the woman in charge. "Whenever you're ready."

He pretended to reach under a chicken and then held up an imaginary egg to an imaginary camera. "Farm fresh goodness from our home to your table," he said with no fake accent. He looked at the imaginary camera, smiled a little bit and gave a slight nod when he finished the line.

"Nice job," said the boss woman. "Is that your real accent?"

"Yes, ma'am." Able answered.

"Oh my God, please don't call me ma'am," she said in apparent agony. "I'm not that old for crying out loud."

"Yes, ma'am," Able said, then caught himself. "I mean, Ok."

Able was taught to say ma'am and sir to anyone much older than him to show respect for his elders. She was at least forty, maybe even forty-five, but she was definitely a ma'am in his book—whether she liked it or not. Everyone in the room, except Able, huddled around the desk and whispered to each other. They nodded back and forth to one another, then the boss woman asked if Able could wait around for a little while longer.

"Yes, ma . . . I mean, ah, sure no problem," he said. "Thank you." Able went back out into the main room with all the other wanna-be's and sat down to wait for a while.

Able had arrived in Los Angeles about three months ago pretty much out of the blue. He was working on a school project during his first semester of college and just got to thinking how he didn't really want to be there at all. He was still pining for Ava and he couldn't concentrate on anything, much less Econ 101. One night, he packed up most of his clothes and the next morning he hit the road. It was a split-second decision with no thought at all about what it would take to move across the country and begin an acting career—much less about how to acquire the real necessities in life, like how to feed himself and pay rent. The crazy thing about it was that he really didn't even want to be an actor. He thought it would be kind of cool, plus he had done really well in his Acting 101 class in summer school and thought, "How hard can it be?" Seriously, the professor thought Able had a "certain look" and "real potential" if he wanted to give it a shot in LA LA Land. Of course, all it took was Able getting a little bored with school, combined with thinking too much about Ava one night. The next day he packed up the Millennium Falcon and set a course for the west coast.

Able hadn't seen Ava since John's Island when she ripped his heart clean out of his chest. That was nearly two years ago. Of course, like a complete dope, he called her a bunch and wrote her several letters the months following the "John's Island incident," as it became known. In the first letter, he poured his heart out to her with every lovey-dovey cliché in the book. It was really quite pathetic. If Able were her, he wouldn't take him back either after reading all that crap. The second letter that he sent a few months after the first one was quite different. He called her every name in the book and, basically, told her if she wanted to live her life as a "fucking slut" then that was just fine by him. The third letter was an apology for the second.

It's not like he followed Ava out to Los Angeles or anything. Actually, she and George never even left South Carolina. They dated for a little while, then broke up for a month or so, and then got back together again. It was one of those on again, off again relationships that Able never really understood.

Ava's mother had called once soon after Able had arrived in LA.

"Able, honey," said Margot Dubose. "This is Mrs. Dubose, how are you?"

"Uh, hey there, Mrs. Dubose," stammered Able. "I'm doing okay, I guess. Uh, how are you and Mr. Dubose doing?"

"Not well, honey," she said in a pleasant, yet sad voice. "I'm afraid we've had to put Ava into a rehabilitation facility in Florida. She'll be there for the next several months to try and get herself together."

"Rehab?" questioned Able. "I know she drinks some, but is this really necessary?"

"Oh, honey, yes," said Mrs. Dubose in her genteel manner. "It's much worse than you know and this has been coming for some time now."

It turned out that Ava had a serious drinking problem for quite a while, even when they were dating, which completely threw Able for a loop. On the nights that they would go out she'd take a shot or two of Vodka before he showed up. So, before they even drank anything together she was already feeling no pain, which explained a lot of her behavior. Seriously, he had no idea she had been drinking when he picked her up all those times. He really just thought she was a fun, slam-ass wild girl, but it turned out she was a fun, slam-ass drunk. You know, she never even seemed drunk even when he knew they were drunk together. He guessed alcoholics knew how to play the part.

Here he had been thinking he was some adorable, irresistible sex machine, but really he was just another idiot horn-dog guy who was being played like a piano by a beautiful alcoholic.

Falling for George again was a real turning point for Ava, because he got her into cocaine. Unfortunately, she loved it. She had one of those addictive personalities that would cling to anything that made her feel good, or make her not feel anything, whichever way you wanted to look at it. Well, cocaine became her drug of choice and it practically ruined her life at twenty. Able didn't blame George, though. If it wasn't him who turned her onto coke it would've been someone else. She was destined to

become a powder queen. She spent six weeks in her first rehab program. When she got out she went right back to George and they got high that very day.

"Able!" one of the audition peons called as they poked their head out from the doorway. "Can you come back in?"

He walked back into the audition room and tried to clear his head of Ava thoughts and remember the line. "From our table to your house," he thought. No, he knew that wasn't it. *Oh, hell,* he thought, *I'm gonna blow it.*

"Able," said the boss woman. "I think you did an excellent job and we would like to offer you the part of Chicken Boy." She stood up and reached her hand out across the desk. "Congratulations."

He took a few steps forward and shook her hand. "That's great," he said without much enthusiasm. "Chicken Boy . . . that's really great."

One of the peons led him to an adjoining room as he thanked the others on his way out with a wave. There were other people in a room next door who took his name and number, then his agent's information. They gave him a complete script and the day, place and time of the shoot. He left after several minutes and headed to his agent's office, although he was not as excited as he expected to be after getting his first gig as an actor.

He thought it would be hard as hell to find an agent in LA, but he was signed within the first two weeks of being there. Of course, he thought that meant he was a great talent or something, but it was really just a numbers game. Volume, volume, volume and hope to hell that one of their little actor wanna-be's hit it big. His real job was working in the basement of Neiman Marcus on Rodeo Drive as a gift wrapper. He actually interviewed to be a salesman in the men's department. They hired him on the spot, then said they needed some help in gift wrapping for just a few days—what a crock. He was still working down in "the dungeon" and it had been three goddamn months.

One of the girls in gift wrapping was an actor too, actually several wrappers were actors, but she was next to his station. It seemed that everyone in LA was an actor no matter what they actually did to pay the rent. She told Able about her agent and how she sent her on cattle calls all the time—that's what they call auditions. So, he called up the agent and got an appointment. Her office was in Century City, which was way the hell away from work and the hell hole where he lived, but he drove out to meet her anyway. Her office was very plush and in a very tall building that stuck out like a sore thumb since there weren't a lot of tall buildings in LA. There was a small earthquake when he was there and he could feel the building sway back and forth a little bit. Of course,

no one did much of anything, since these things probably happened all the time, but it scared the living shit out of Able.

The agent called him in her office and they talked for about ten minutes. She liked his "look" and thought she could get him some stand-in work for several known actors. He didn't know what stand-in work was, but at least it was work.

"Well," the agent said looking Able up and down. "We'll need to change your name . . . something catchy and memorable. One or two syllables only. That makes it easier for the public to remember you." She started spouting off names of well-known actors. She enunciated each syllable and flashed one, or one-two with her fingers for each name; like Dus-tin Hoff-man, Paul New-man, Hen-ry Fon-da. She went on and on to name like twenty actors, who all obviously had successful careers because they didn't exceed her two syllable rule. He guessed no real talent was required.

Once there was a pause in her long list of names he looked at her and said, "A-ble Cur-ran." He held up his hand and counted the syllables on his fingers as he spoke. She saw through the sarcasm and didn't appreciate it too much. She said they would need to work on it, his name that is, not the sarcasm.

She handed him a sheet of paper with a bunch of single words on it and some lines from various plays. She asked him to read through the list. After a few minutes of reading the words and lines she stopped him.

"That's enough," she barked. "I'll have to get you into voice lessons. That accent is way to Southern to make it in this business."

"Well," he said, still being a bit sarcastic. "This is how I talk, like it or not. I can do other accents if you want, but I'm not changing my normal accent."

He started reading the lines from the sheet of paper using a proper English accent, then a Cockney accent, then a Brooklyn accent. She looked at him and nodded her head.

"Not bad," she said. "Not bad at all. Okay, I think I can work with you."

She started sending him on auditions within just a few days, which was exciting. Although the auditions were mostly for small-time jobs, it made him feel like he was really an actor, which was kind of cool.

He finally got to his agent's office to tell her about the grocery store commercial audition. Her secretary told him to go on in since she was expecting him. He walked through the doorway and she stood up from behind her desk and began to clap her hands.

“All right, Chicken Boy!” she said all excited. “Today it’s a grocery store commercial, tomorrow it’s the Academy Awards.”

Chapter Twenty-One

Charleston, South Carolina

—March 1983—

The early morning sun pierced through the small openings of the old Venetian blinds in a dingy, stale apartment. A sun beam cut across Ava's face and woke her from a fitful sleep. She tried to raise her arm to shade her eyes, but couldn't move. She squinted hard as she took in her surroundings and realized she was in a strange place. A naked man lay across the bed with his head on her bare stomach. Ava realized she was tied to the four corners of the bed with torn sheets and had no idea how she came to be in this predicament. She began to flail her arms and legs about screaming to be turned loose.

"All right, all right," said the naked man after being jostled awake. "I'll untie you, just shut up. I have a mother of a hangover."

"Who the hell are you?" asked Ava, upset at being tied down with absolutely no control over the situation.

"Don't tell me you can't remember," said the naked man, now untying the knotted sheets around Ava's legs and wrists. "I'm Frank. I know we were fucked up, but you've got to remember how great that was last night. I'll be telling this story for years."

Ava looked at Frank and tried to recall the events of the last twenty four hours. He was nice looking with a shaved head, a gold loop earring in each ear and tattoos covering both arms and his shoulders. She scanned down his muscular body past the pierced nipples and just beyond his flat, toned stomach. She realized the only hair on his body was under his arms. The rest of him was shaved clean as a whistle. He stood before her with his penis drawn in like a scared turtle and the tell-tale red bumps of a recent shave.

"You did a pretty good job," said Frank noticing where she was looking. He rubbed his hand over his shaved crotch. "That's the way you like it, right?"

"Get me outta here," said Ava, disgusted as she finally got to her feet. "I don't remember a fucking thing—and if I don't remember it, then it didn't happen."

"Oh, it happened," said Frank, now getting excited at his conquest. "You've got to be the nastiest bitch I've ever met—man, you are fucking insane—and I've known some real freak shows in my day."

Chapter 21

Ava searched the room for her clothes and piled them on the bed before getting dressed. She didn't notice anything different until she was pulling up her underpants—she stepped toward Frank and punched him in the chest.

"You fucking shaved me!" she screamed. "You asshole!"

"It was your idea!" Frank yelled back. "You shaved me, then wanted me to shave you—it was your fucking idea. The whole 'tie me up' thing was your idea. 'Tie me up and hurt me' you said. You begged me to do all kinds of shit—I was just going along for the ride. Man, you're a crazy bitch!"

Ava was only wearing enough clothes to cover her nakedness when she stormed out into the cold, early morning. She finished getting dressed on the concrete stoop of the student apartment house somewhere in Clemson, South Carolina. The night had begun at her local watering hole in Charleston—a good three hours away. She had no idea how she had gotten this far or what else had happened that night, although her sore legs and multiple bruises gave a hint of her nocturnal activities.

She walked six blocks before finding a pay phone at a 24-hour diner. She knew the number by heart and a sleepy, gruff voice answered on the second ring. He accepted the reversed charges.

"I'll be there as soon as I can, sweetie," said the kind, understanding voice. "You get some breakfast and I'll take care of the bill when I get there. I love you, sweetie."

"I love you too, Daddy," said Ava as she wiped away a tear.

Ava hung up the phone and huddled in the corner of the phone booth. She fought back the tears as best as she could, but they began to flow down her cheeks in a river of sadness. *Why do I do these things*, she thought. *What's wrong with me? God help me . . . please God . . . please God . . . help me.* She buried her head in her hands and sobbed.

The door to the phone booth swung open and Ava looked up to see an outstretched hand. "Come on, sweetie," said her father. "It'll be all right."

Ava had been crouched in the phone booth and crying for hours. She stood up and hugged her father tightly. She was shaking uncontrollably. He held her for a long time while repeatedly whispering, "I love you, sweetie," in her ear. Once she settled down a bit they both went inside the diner for coffee and another father-daughter talk.

Mr. Dubose ordered the Country Man Special of three eggs over easy, bacon, toast, a short stack of buttermilk pancakes with orange juice and coffee. Ava had coffee only—black. She steadied her cup with both hands and took small sips. She cried quietly as her father spoke of her going back to rehab again. It would be her third time in two years. This time it would be for months, however, not weeks.

"I don't know what else to do, sweetie," said her father, holding back his emotions. "I'll pay any amount of money to get you better, but you have to want it. You have to make a commitment to your mother and me. Please, sweetie. I can't stand to see you this way." He choked back the tears. "Just look at you. You're slowly killing yourself."

He placed a hand over his eyes and turned away. Showing emotion was a sign of weakness to Mr. Dubose and he would not be seen as a weak man. He cleared his throat and blinked away any possible tears.

"I'm sorry, Daddy," she said through quiet tears and reached for his hand. "I'll go back. I'll go back and try to make you proud of me."

"I'm already proud of you, sweetie," said Mr. Dubose, sniffling. "This time go back to make you proud of you."

"I can never be proud of myself, Daddy," said Ava. "I'm a junkie and a fuck up. What's there to be proud of? I mean, look at me, Daddy. What's there to be proud of?"

"There's a good soul inside you, sweetie," said her father as he reached across the table and hugged Ava's neck. His shirt now dripping with Pure Maple Syrup and melted butter, but he was oblivious. "You find that goodness to share with others and you'll be proud. Believe me, sweetie, you'll be proud."

Ava held onto her father tightly and spoke through the tears.

"I'll find the good in me, Daddy," she whispered in his ear. "I'll find the good."

Chapter Twenty Two

Los Angeles, California

—June 1984—

One of the steps in the twelve step program of AA is to apologize to those who you've hurt in some way. Able was not sure what all the other steps were about, but that one stupid step would turn his life upside down.

He was living in this crappy little studio apartment on Rose Avenue in Venice Beach. It was basically one room with a kitchenette behind a curtain on one wall and a tiny bathroom jammed in the corner. Now he knew where all the jokes came from about taking a crap and a shower at the same time. Seriously, it could have been easily done in this place.

Even though the place was a dump, it was cheap and just three blocks off the beach—and all the crazies on the boardwalk of Venice Beach. People go on and on about how great Southern California is, which might be true if

you're only talking about the weather, but the city streets are just as filthy as anywhere in New York City. There are bums all over the place who don't think twice about taking a leak in the alley or sleeping on your stoop with their trash bags full of possessions. Able guessed that kind of stuff got edited out by the department of tourism.

It was nearly midnight and Able was lying on this ratty old couch that came with the apartment. He was watching *The Tonight Show* on a twelve inch color TV with a bad vertical hold. It drove him nuts watching the picture hover at mid-screen every thirty seconds before righting itself again, but he couldn't afford a new TV. The phone rang with a loud, clattering old-timey bell ring. It was the phone he brought with him from school, which was white with a purple and gold "Go Pirates" sticker on the receiver. He was sure it was his mother calling to tell him something like his second cousin twice removed had died or that her camellia was starting to bloom. Something earth shattering for sure.

"Yeellloow," Able said answering the phone feeling kind of goofy. "Denny's Dog Den, they poop, we scoop. Can I help ya?"

"Honey Bun?" a sweet voice said nervously. "Is that you?"

It had been over a year since he last spoke with Ava, and hearing her voice again took his breath away. He sat silent for a good ten seconds as his heart pounded in his chest, while he tried to take a few deep breaths to help compose himself.

"Ava, hey there," he said, completely flustered. "How are you doing? How'd you get this number?"

"It's so good to hear your voice again," said Ava without answering his questions. "You're still a bit of a nut aren't you?" She laughed that sexy laugh.

"Oh, just goofing off a little," he said. "I really thought you were my mother. You're the last person on earth I thought would be calling me."

"Well, I did get your number from your mother," she said. "I had to really convince her to give it to me, too. I'm afraid she doesn't like me very much after everything that's gone on. I don't really blame her, though."

"I'm really kind of busy, so I can't talk long," he said in kind of a rude tone. "I've got a big day tomorrow, so, what can I do for you?"

Ava told him about how she was supposed to apologize to those she hurt when she was drinking and drugging before she could continue on with the other steps in the AA program. She was released a few weeks earlier from a rehab facility in South Carolina for the third time in two years. One part of the recovery was that she attended local AA meetings several times a week—or every day if necessary. She had been going every day for the past two weeks since the temptation for her was so great. Everyone at the meeting was there to support one another and keep their fellow alcoholics or addicts on the path of sobriety. According to Ava, she needed all the support she could get, since the bottle and the powder were continuously calling out to her.

"I know that I hurt you, Able," she said in her soft Southern accent that had him melting already. "The person that hurt you wasn't me though, not the real me. It was a demon that formed inside me when I was drinking and drugging. A demon I had no control over. It made me hurt the people I love the most."

Ava's voice began to quiver. She paused briefly and took a deep breath. Tears welled up in Able's eyes at the sound of her getting emotional, and the fact that there was nothing he could do to help just killed him. He sat there and held the phone to his ear and wiped away tears before they made it too far down his cheeks.

"I'm asking you to forgive me, Able," she said choking back tears. "I need your forgiveness more than anyone else—you mean more to me than anyone on this earth."

Now the tears rolled down his cheeks faster than he could wipe them away, so he just let them roll. He bit his lower lip and tried to gather himself to speak, but he simply couldn't form any words. His chest heaved with emotion and the tears continued to flow. He could hear

Ava on the other end of the phone crying and sniffling. He was sure she heard the same from him. They both held their phones, but didn't speak a word. They were comforted by the fact that even with over 2,500 miles between them, there was still a connection. They must have sat there and cried for ten minutes without a word between them. Finally, he composed himself just long enough to speak.

"I forgive you, Ava," he said, then quickly hung up the phone.

He began to sob uncontrollably and fell face first onto his stinky, old couch. All the feelings he felt before and all the heartache from the break-up crashed down on him in one tidal wave of emotion that he could not hold back. His body heaved and convulsed as he cried harder than any other time in his life.

He cried himself to sleep and woke up on the couch as rays of sunlight streamed in through the tattered blinds. It was another beautiful day in Southern California, but all he could think about was getting back to Ava.

Chapter Twenty-Three

Charleston, South Carolina

—July 1984—

The bell above the Waffle House door dinged loudly as Ava and her friends from AA left after their usual post-meeting cup of decaf. The casual gathering gave them time to talk one on one about how each of them was doing and to gain some additional strength from friends. Ava had been going to meetings three days a week since her last stay in rehab. She felt good about her progress, but the demons constantly whispered in her ear. As any alcoholic or addict will tell you . . . "take it one day at a time."

"See you in a few days," Ava called to her group of friends as she opened her car door. "I love you all, be strong!"

"Bye, sweetie," one called out. "Love you too. Don't forget to call me with that family chicken dish recipe. Bye, bye!"

Everyone drove off to their respective homes after checking off another day of sobriety.

Ava slipped into her nightgown, a short cotton pull-over that hung just above her knees. The short sleeves and neck line were adorned with needlepoint detail of pink roses with light green stems and leaves. The water kettle whistled hot and she prepared some Chamomile tea to help her fall asleep. She curled up in bed with her tea and the big fall preview issue of *Vogue.*

It was close to midnight when Ava turned off her bed-side lamp, pulled the covers up to her chin and melted into her goose down mattress. She barely had time to fall asleep when there was a loud banging on her front door.

"Hey, baby!" howled a familiar voice. "Santa Claus is coming early this year, so open up!" *Bang, bang, bang.* "Come on, baby, open up!"

Ava jumped from her bed and ran downstairs to open the front door. "Get in here!" she demanded softly, grab-bing George's arm. "You're going to wake up the whole damn complex."

George staggered into the living room of Ava's new condo in Mt. Pleasant, just north of Charleston. Her father had bought it for her months earlier to try and give her some stability . . . without living under his own roof. It was a simple place, but nice. Two bedrooms and two bathrooms upstairs with a living room, kitchen and half-bath downstairs. There was a pool for owners to enjoy in the warmer months and a clubhouse for "socials" in the winter. The complex was a good mix of older folks who were downsizing now that their kids were grown and young folks just getting started. Ava recognized a few of her fellow condo owners at AA meetings recently, but they didn't speak of it at the complex among mixed company, the sober set.

"What in the hell are you doing here," said Ava with hands on her hips. Her rosy nipples were visible as her bosoms pressed against the thin cotton night gown. "You know I've been clean for nearly four months now. I don't want you here. I don't need you here."

"If you're a good little girl," George said rubbing the back of his hand across Ava's chest. "Then Santa has some presents for you."

He laughed his creepy laugh as Ava slapped his hand away. She crossed her arms across her chest to cover any temptation.

"Don't be a bitch, Ava, it's Georgie boy," he said. "And looky, looky what I've got for us."

George reached into the pocket of his tattered barn jacket and pulled out two clear baggies. One was a quarter full of cocaine and the other had a mix of blue, black and white pills. George held a baggie in each hand and danced in front of Ava. "Looky, looky what I have," he sang, like a little boy teasing a friend.

"God damn you, George," she said, frustrated. "You know I can't be near that shit. I'm holding on by a fucking thread here and you bring that shit into my house. God damn you!"

"Oh, baby," George said as he put his arms around Ava's neck, still holding the baggies. "You know I love you, don't you?" He kissed her sweetly on the forehead.

"I love you, too, George, but I can't do this. I can't." She leaned her head on his shoulder and sighed. "It's just so hard on a normal day and now you're holding coke and pills a foot away from me. I can't take it. This is why I've stayed away from you the last year. You are the last person I need to see."

George stepped back and scanned the room. "Baby," he said. "I think you're stronger than you know. A little bump ain't gonna kill ya. It might even be what you need to take the edge off."

He saw a small mirror across the room and took it off the wall. He sat on the sofa and poured half the baggie out and began cutting the coke into lines with a credit card.

"George!" Ava yelled. "No, this is not happening!"

George licked his finger and pressed it in the coke. He stood up and walked over to Ava. "Believe me, baby," he said sliding his finger into Ava's mouth. "You can handle this, you're strong."

George rubbed the coke on Ava's gums as she stood there motionless, letting the demons back in. The coke made her gums tingle and her lips went numb. Suddenly, she took his hand and thrust his finger deep into her mouth. She sucked the remaining cocaine off his finger, then grabbed his face with both hands and kissed him hard. They fell to the floor kissing madly, rolling about and pulling off each other's clothes.

Moments later they stopped. Sex is secondary to addicts, so Ava and George broke their clench and crawled to the coffee table. Ava kneeled in front of the lines of coke like she was about to receive communion. George pulled a dollar bill out of his pocket and rolled it tight. He handed it to Ava who leaned in to snort three of the four lines before handing it back over for George to have a turn. He didn't care. He had plenty to go around.

Ava lay back on the living room rug, topless and only wearing her cotton underpants. She buried her face in her hands and felt a surge of guilt and sadness. "What the hell am I doing," she moaned. She breathed in deeply, then let it out with a big sigh. The moment passed and she knelt again at the coffee table before her master.

She took the dollar bill from George, leaned down and snorted her fourth line in two minutes. She had fallen again and couldn't control the tumble.

It was four in the morning when they decided to take a ride. The coke in the baggie was all gone, they'd each popped a few quaaludes and they'd had all the sex they could stand for one night. They were too wired to sleep, so they decided to take a drive in the country.

They climbed into George's black Range Rover LWB with dark tinted windows and every extra the dealer offered. George rarely went off-road; he really bought it for the panache rather than the utility.

Weeks earlier, George had a terrible wreck in his Mercedes sedan when he failed to see a stop sign at a "T" in the road and ran straight into a two-hundred-year-old Live Oak in old Charleston. He walked away with a broken pinky finger and the underage girl he was with broke both legs. His lawyers cleaned up the legal mess, paid off the girl's family and somehow kept George from losing his license.

The next day George walked into Low Country Range Rover and picked out his new ride. When asked how he wanted to finance the deal, George just laughed and placed his American Express black card on the salesman's desk. He drove away thirty minutes later after signing the AMEX slip for $65,000.

George and Ava headed out on Ashley River Road through some of the most beautiful and storied countryside in the south. There were several notable plantations that dotted the landscape out that way: Drayton Hall, Magnolia Plantation and Middleton Place. George turned off the headlights and pulled into the entrance to the Middleton Equestrian Center. He stopped at the old gate held up by century-old bricks and mortar. He breathed in a lung full of smoke, then flicked the cigarette into the sandy soil. The Equestrian Center was part of the larger Middleton Place Plantation grounds where the horses were kept when not lugging a carriage full of sunburned tourists. The Center also leased out stalls to the public who train and show at the facility.

“What are you doing, George?” questioned Ava, stepping one foot out of the Rover. “Let’s keep driving. It’s a beautiful night.”

“I want to ride a horsey,” said George, laughing his creepy laugh. “Come on, let’s go, baby! Don’t you want to ride a horsey?”

Before Ava could respond, George was out of the car and jumped the front gate. He began running across the rutty driveway, through the front paddock and toward the barns in the distance. Ava rolled her eyes, but then jumped out to follow. She climbed over the gate and fell on the other side. She ran across the well-worn driveway calling quietly for George to slow down.

She caught up to him at the first barn where he stopped to catch his breath. "George, let's get outta here," she said, short of breath herself. "We're going to get caught."

"Don't worry, baby," said George as he pushed her against the barn and kissed her hard. "I've got it all under control. This way."

George led the way to a larger barn about fifty yards away. He pushed on the large gate and it squeaked open just enough for him and Ava to slide through. Once inside, they looked around the huge building that housed twenty-five horses of all shapes and sizes. A tack area in the corner of the barn stored bits, stirrups and other equestrian gear. Grooming brushes and blankets were neatly placed on nearby shelves. They walked past the stalls admiring the horses and read their nameplates aloud to each other.

"Aunt Trudie's Shoes," called out Ava with a laugh. "Palmetto Miracle, Angel of My Soul, GetReadyGo," *and I'm the one on drugs*, she thought to herself.

The sound of horses breathing deeply and a few whinnies showed their sense that something was not right.

"This one is mine," said George in a whisper looking at a huge Warm Blood that had to be eighteen hands tall. "Come here, beauty. Let's go for a little ride."

George unclasped the gate and walked slowly into stall

number 8. The horse was big and beautiful, light gray in color with a few black flecks on his haunch. He was backing up and snorting, his ears straight back and his eyes wide.

"George," said Ava in a concerned tone. "Leave him alone. Let's get outta here. Please, leave him alone."

"Shut up and get you own horse," said George in a mean whisper. "I'm not leaving until I get my ride."

George stepped closer and closer. He held his hands up to try and calm the animal. He finally reached the horse and patted his nose and rubbed his long gray neck.

"That's right, boy," said George softly. "That's right. I'm your friend. It's okay. Let's just go for a little ride. That's right."

George tried to lead the horse out the stall, but he was tentative and shook his head up and down. "Easy boy," said George. "Come on. It's okay. Come on."

Ava backed up as the huge horse walked slowly out of the stall. Even in the dim light she could see his strength rippling with each step and the regal air of his gait.

"Help me hold him still while I get on," said George, now moving toward the side of the horse. "I'll use this step stool, then hop on."

"George, let's put him back," Ava pleaded. "Please, let's put him back and just go home. Please."

“Shut the fuck up and hold him,” said George, now tired of the whining. “I’m going to ride this fucking horse, so just shut up.”

George was on the top of the step stool with one hand holding tightly to the mane and the other on the horse’s back. Ava reached up to pat the horse’s neck and did her best to hold him steady.

“Geronimo!” yelled George as he leaped off the stool and onto the horse’s back. He grabbed the horse’s mane with both hands and held on tight. The horse bounced up and down off the ground quickly with his front legs and snorted.

“Easy, boy,” said Ava still stroking his nose and jaw. “Easy now.”

Without warning, George kicked the horse hard with both heels, which sent him rearing up on his back legs. Ava did not have time to react as the horse towered over her, kicking his front legs and snorting loud. In an instant, the horse came down, then reared up again quickly. One of his front hooves caught Ava under the chin and sent her reeling. She banged into the stall and crumbled to the concrete floor. Blood oozed from under her chin, mouth and nose. A red pool formed around her face as she lay there unconscious. The horse reared up again and came down on Ava’s leg. The force snapped her femur in two like a twig. She didn't feel anything though; she was out cold.

"Whoa, boy, whoa," yelled George. He jumped from his mount and the horse trotted down to the other end of the stable. He stood in the far corner and snorted, then slapped his hoof at the ground.

George knelt down beside Ava and brushed her hair back with his hand. "Baby, can you hear me," he said. "Baby, get up. I'm sorry, baby. I'm sorry."

Ava did not move. George could see that she was breathing, but didn't know what to do. Suddenly, he saw a thin flash of light at the barn door where they entered and heard the slam of a screen door across the barn yard.

George ran to the barn door and peered out. He saw the silhouette of a man walking down the porch steps from the small caretaker house. George panicked. He looked back at Ava, then turned quickly and slid through the barn door. "Hey, you!" someone called. George didn't stop. He sprinted across the front paddock and leaped over the front gate. He started the Rover and slammed the pedal into the floor. The tires spun for a moment and threw sand into air, squealing against the pavement as George made a hard u-turn. He drove well out of sight before turning on his headlights to head back to Charleston.

Chapter Twenty-Four

Los Angeles, California

—July 1984—

The jerk in the bad toupee and cheesy suit sent his steak back for the second time. "Now it's over done," he said with a card-carrying LA asshole flair. "Don't you know how to cook a Goddamn steak?"

"Yes sir, I do," Able said a bit sarcastically. "However, I'm just the waiter here, not the chef. He wears the big poofy hat and works back in the kitchen area." Able gestured with his hands to indicate "poofy hat" and pointed. The guest didn't find his theatrics very amusing.

"Where's the manager!" he yelled. "I demand to see the manager!"

The manager heard the commotion from across the room and was already on his way. He walked quickly to the table. "Yes, is there a problem here?"

"You're damn right there's a problem," said the jerk, who was now embarrassing his whole table. "Your little snot of a waiter first brought me my steak too rare and now it's overcooked. I want this whole meal comped or I'll never eat here again. Do you know who I am?"

"Don't comp this guy's meal, Bill," Able said to his manager, tired of the bullshit. "I've been dealing with his shit for the past forty-five minutes. He's a no-class, second-rate producer and a throbbing dickhead. Don't let jerks like this run our lives, man."

"You little shit," the jerk stood up and threw down his napkin. "I want this little shit fired, do you hear me, fired!"

Bill just looked at Able and that was all it took. "Ok, Ok, I'm gone," Able said holding back a smile. "But the day you let dickheads like this run your life, well, then it's time to change your life." He leaned over the only cute girl at the table and grabbed a warm, fresh roll from the basket of bread with one hand and the half-full bottle of Pinot Noir with the other.

"What are they going to do . . . fire me twice?" Able said to the cute blonde at the table. "Want to join me? It's much more fun where I'm going." She just smiled and shook her head no, but he could tell that she really wanted to leave.

It really wasn't more fun where he was going. Maybe it would have been if the cute girl from the jerk's table actually joined him. He was happy to get home to his crappy apartment though, and finish off the wine in front of a little late night television. It was the third time he'd been fired in a year and his impatience with jerk customers and LA in general was showing. He had been getting some commercial acting gigs that paid pretty well, but not enough to quit his serving jobs. Waiting tables was the best supplement for any wanna-be actor, since the hours were flexible with others willing to trade shifts. He needed to get discovered soon, though, so he could stop getting fired.

The last thing he remembered was David Letterman blowing him a kiss. He hit the off button on the remote control and staggered off to bed.

He woke up early the next morning and studied his lines over a hot cup of coffee. He had a third callback for a movie called, *Sweet Tea*, a modern day *Gone With The Wind.* It was a small part, but at least it was a feature film and not some local yokel commercial. His first two readings went really well and he was excited to have the chance to read for a third time. This time the actual director and producers would be there. The part should be his unless he just completely blew it.

He rushed to get ready, then headed out to the bus stop, since the bus took forever to get anywhere. He was planning on an hour door to door and that was with two transfers. The Millennium Falcon died a few weeks ago and he really didn't have the money for another junker.

He had been cruising down the Pacific Coast highway from Huntington Beach back up to LA. when the month-long rattling stopped. He thought the car had fixed itself until he heard a big clang and then saw engine parts bouncing down the highway. He coasted to a stop, got out and lifted the hood. He was not sure what he was looking for since he had no idea how an engine worked, apart from putting in the gas and oil. He could tell some major parts were missing as smoke billowed from the engine. Music was important to him, so he gathered up all his tapes and pulled the new Kenwood stereo out of the dashboard, then the new speakers from the doors and backseat. Luckily, an old duffle bag was in the way back and he stuffed it full of valuables . . . jumper cables, some t-shirts, his tennis racket and several loose tennis balls. The last thing he took from the car was the license plate. He scribbled "LA" on a piece of cardboard, threw the duffle bag over one shoulder and extended his thumb.

After about ten minutes a car full of kids returning from Tijuana pulled over and gave him a lift most of the way home.

Chapter Twenty-Five

Charleston, South Carolina

—July 1984—

"She only wants to see you," said Mrs. Dubose, dabbing a tear with a silk handkerchief. "I'm so grateful to you for coming." She reached out and took his hand, then pulled him close and held on tight. "You're a good man, Able Curran," she whispered as she squeezed him tightly.

Mr. Dubose walked over and touched his shoulder. It was the most affection Able had witnessed from him in ten years.

"I don't know who else would fly clear across the country for someone like Ava, but I sure am grateful," he said in a gentlemanly southern drawl. "We've done all we know to do, but it's just never been enough."

He paused for a moment as reality set in. "What else can

I do to save my baby girl?" he said, now getting choked up. "Tell me, Able, after four rehabs, private therapy, trying to buy her sobriety with condos and cars. What else can I do?"

Mr. Dubose quickly turned and walked a few steps down the stark white corridor. He slowly wiped his eyes with both hands and ran his fingers through his thick, graying hair. Mrs. Dubose went to console her husband. Their eyes locked on each other for a moment, then they reached out to one another and held each other for what seemed like forever. Virtual strangers for the last several years, the Duboses recaptured their love for one another in the midst of tragedy. Their struggle to save Ava's life made their marriage troubles seem so petty. Once they came to that realization, their love for one another began to blossom again. They needed someone to lean on and, once again, they were there for each other.

Able watched Ava's parents, who had tried so hard to help their daughter, at a loss for what to do next.

"She'll be all right," Able said, trying to give them a ray of hope. "I think this accident may be the wake-up call that she needs. Don't worry, she'll get through this, we'll all get through this."

Able kissed Mrs. Dubose on the cheek and reached out to shake Mr. Dubose's hand. He pulled Able in for an unexpected bear hug, then gently patted his face. Their faces were splotchy and tear streaked. Their eyes were tired and swollen from little to no sleep over the last twenty-four hours.

"Try to get some rest," Able said, smiling at them both. He then pushed through the door at Room 214 at Charleston Memorial where Ava lay fighting to stay alive.

Ava had been found by the caretaker of the Middleton Plantation Equestrian Center, who called the police and paramedics. She had a broken jaw, several shattered teeth and a compound fracture of her right femur, but the worst injury was a broken neck. They thought the initial blow by the horse's hoof broke her jaw, teeth and her neck at the same time. The leg was broken when the horse stomped on her after rearing up again. Luckily, the owners of the ranch did not press charges against Ava. They figured she learned her lesson with a good year of physical therapy in front of her, if she survived at all. They did, however, want to throw the book at the cowardly boy who ran away, but Ava wouldn't talk. For some reason she was protecting the only other person who had done as much to ruin her life as she had.

Ava's mother called Able the morning of the accident and gave him a brief account of what happened. The most unsettling news was when she told him they only gave Ava a twenty-five percent chance to live because of the location of the broken neck. He dropped everything and was on the next flight from Los Angeles to Charleston, South Carolina.

That was less than twenty-four hours ago. Now, he was standing in Ava's room looking at the most beautiful woman he had ever known…even though her entire face and head were a purplish-blue with white bandages covering the multiple stitches in her chin. She had bolts through her forehead that held the halo in place, so her neck was immobilized. Her right leg was in a cast from upper thigh to her ankle. It too was stark white with none of the usual salutations. *Still beautiful*, he thought.

There were flashing monitors on the wall and beside the bed. Each one beeping or pulsing the fact that Ava was still alive, but just barely. A morphine drip hung to the left of the bed and slowly sent the soothing drug down a tube and into Ava's veins. He looked around at all the science and thanked God that it was here to save her. He had never seen someone that he loved in that condition before and he was overwhelmed by the magnitude of the situation. He gently took Ava's hand and sobbed quietly at the prospect of losing her again, and for good. *She can't see me this upset*, he told himself. *Be strong, you wimp*. He paused for a second to compose himself and wiped away the tears.

"Ava," he called out quietly. "Ava, you awake?" He leaned in closer. "Ava, can you hear me?"

Ava's eyes began to flutter. She squinted at the light of the room, then looked around to see who was there. The halo was so restrictive that he had to lean completely over her, so she could see his face. Their eyes met for the first time in years and he smiled to try and give her hope.

"Hey, honey bun," he said with a smile. "Isn't this a bit extreme just to get me back to the east coast?"

Ava smiled with her eyes, as tears welled up and rolled down her bruised cheeks. Her mouth curled ever so slightly as she tried to smile. Her jaw was wired shut and she looked a mess, but he could read her eyes. They were still blue and beautiful. She could tell him anything with just one look. He heard her loud and clear. He reached out and held her hand. She squeezed his hand tightly as the tears began to flow.

"It'll be all right, honey bun," Able said sweetly. "You just rest up, now. It'll be all right, I'm here." He leaned down and kissed her hand, then reached over and gently wiped the tears off her bruised cheek. Ava looked at him intently, then closed her eyes, exhausted by the sixty-second visit, and fell back to sleep.

He pulled a pen out of his pocket and was the first to sign her cast. He signed it about mid-thigh, so Ava could read it.

It read: "The delicious Able Curran was here."

Chapter Twenty-Six

Charleston, South Carolina

—November 1984—

The apartment in Charleston was just as crappy as the one in LA, but at least it was closer to Ava. It came fully furnished with a single bed jammed in one corner and a small bedside table and lamp. The sheets were dank and musty with a design that screamed 1975. In the far corner, near the only window, was a sink and old medicine cabinet . . . old enough to have a slot in the tile for used razor blades. The small, round sink was mostly white, but plenty of rust-colored stains showed its seventy-five years of service with lead-heavy water. The family of roaches that lived in the wall behind the sink only came out at night. Able and the family had an understanding and kept to themselves.

The new place was on the seedier side of King Street near Calhoun Street and the College of Charleston. It was

above a bakery, so there were fresh muffins and breads each morning. During the first few weeks, Able would rise late, still on LA time, grab a copy of the *Charleston Post* and *Courier,* sit at the corner table and ease into the morning with a fresh blueberry muffin and coffee. There was nothing quite like the smell of a true bakery first thing in the morning. Muffins, pastries, hard rolls, cannolis and baguettes lay stacked in the glass case. The aroma was magical and filled every inch of the small bakery. There were several tables inside and two outside on the sidewalk, one at each window. The green, white and red Italian flag was painted on each window with "A Taste of Italy" in script underneath. The shop was bustling from 6:00 a.m. until 9:00 a.m., then the crowd slowed to a crawl with the random late sleepers and students that stumbled in before class.

Able usually arrived at the hospital mid-morning once Ava was already up and preparing for her daily round of physical therapy. The doctors had been amazed at her recovery and said it was a miracle that she survived at all, much less that she was talking and walking already . . . and bitching. An alcoholic and addict in mid-detox was no fun to be around.

It had been three months of nothing but sleeping, eating and visiting Ava. He knew early on that he would be in Charleston for the long haul, so he had a friend in LA ship the rest of his clothes back east. His friend fit everything he owned in a college-style trunk and secured it with duct tape. Of course, he included his dirty clothes in the package, so when Able opened the trunk at his new place a plume of stale funk rose to fill the room. Once he sifted through his life's possessions he realized that none of it was worth the price of shipping. He pulled out his favorite t-shirt, one with a silhouette of Michael Jordan in mid-soar, then threw away everything else.

Several mornings each week, Able laced-up his well-worn running shoes and headed out for a nice jog. Three miles was about his maximum, or he'd hurl blueberry muffin and coffee all over the city streets. It was a nice diversion though, as he ran down King Street toward White Point Gardens and the Battery. Even in the early morning he'd pass horses pulling carriages as they clomped along the cobblestoned streets with eager tourists snapping photos and listening to their guide's history lesson of this grand southern city. Able could usually make it down to the Battery in full jog, but he slowed to a modestly-paced walk along the East Battery to take in the beauty of the harbor.

Water slapped against the old bulkhead with mounds of oysters clinging to the deteriorating concrete. He could see Fort Sumter in the distance, which was wrestled back from the Union command during the Civil War. Once back in Confederate hands, Fort Sumter protected Charleston Harbor and the city that was the pride of the South, until the end of the war in 1865. The beautiful southern mansions in shades of blue, salmon and green still lined the South Battery and were a reminder of the glory of Charleston and its wealth. His short walk returned to a full jog as he headed back towards his apartment, passing homes with ornate wrought iron gates and secret gardens behind cobbled walls. The *clomp, clomp, clomp* of horse hooves and the booming voice of a tour guide echoed through the narrow streets of lower Broad, King and Meeting.

As he approached the end of his run, the scenery changed from mansions and antique shops to run-down student housing and head shops. The melodic tones of horse hooves were now replaced by the thump, thump, thump of bass blaring from a corner gathering.

Mrs. Spagnoli, the bakery owner, and Able had become fast friends. They chatted during his morning order and, after the morning rush, she joined him for a cup of coffee at the corner table. He had told her all about Ava and her accident. He left out some stuff, but she had the gist of the situation. Italians relish a good love story.

"You must be this girl's *angelo custode*," she said with a strong Italian accent and gestured madly. "For you to drop everything in your life for her tells me that you are very special, very special person."

"In inglese per favore?" he asked.

"Her *angelo custode*," the words rolled off her Italian-born tongue. "Her guardian angel, Able. You must be her guardian angel."

"Well, I don't know about that," he said rather sheepishly. "If I were her guardian angel, then I don't think she'd be in the hospital with a broken neck. I do feel drawn to look out for her, though, and I feel guilty that this happened. I don't know why, I mean, there's nothing I could have done to prevent it, but I still feel guilty."

"Well, I know you're special," said Mrs. Spagnoli, reaching across the table to grab his cheek. "Oh, if I was only thirty years younger, you would be my *angelo*." She patted his cheek lovingly and smiled. "*Il mio ragazzo speciale*," my special boy, she said in her sexy Italian accent. "*Il mio ragazzo speciale*."

He watched Mrs. Spangoli push herself up from the table and stroll to behind the counter. She was the sexiest sixty-year-old that he had ever known. One would never know that she had been up since 3:00 a.m. to start her day. Each morning when Able arrived she looked like she was ready for a date, with her dark hair pulled back in a bun and her brown eyes sparkling. She loved life and it showed in everything she did, from baking her pastries to greeting each customer. She had an hourglass figure with a large chest and curvy hips, maybe a bit overweight, but it all landed in the right spots. The men who frequented her shop did like her baked goods, but they came in just to see her, too. She liked to flirt with the men and it made them feel good. Almost all of her regular customers were greeted with an Italian-style kiss. "*Buon giorno*," she said with excitement. "And how are we on this lovely day." Then smooch, smooch. Her love for life was infectious.

She placed several muffins and pastries into a paper bag and folded the top over to keep in the warmth. She handed them to Able as he stood at the doorway. "Give these to your *angelo,*" she said. "They are better than anything she can get in that hospital." She kissed him on his left cheek, then the right. "Go now, you go to your love," she said pushing him out the door.

"*Amore rende la vita degna di essere vissuta,*" Love makes life worth living, she shouted as Able strolled down the sidewalk. "*Viva l'amore!*"

Chapter Twenty-Seven

Charleston, South Carolina

—January 1985—

The nurse heard the alarm and quickly jumped up and ran down the hallway to room 214. Ava was sitting up in bed and continued to push the red button even as the nurse was catching her breath after the thirty-yard sprint.

"Are you okay, Ava?" she gasped. "What's the matter?"

"Where the hell have you been!" Ava barked. "What kind of hospital is this that would leave a person lying here in pain?"

The nurse checked the morphine drip and it looked fine. The bag was still half full and the dose was what the doctor ordered.

"Where does it hurt?" the nurse asked touching Ava gently on the shoulder.

"Everywhere you bitch!" Ava screamed. "I need more morphine. I'm in pain here. Can't you understand that, or are you as stupid as you look?"

"I'll check with the doctor and do whatever he suggests," said the nurse matter of factly. She turned and walked out the room before she said something that she may regret as Ava continued to scream obscenities.

Able walked up to the nurses' station with two bags of pastries from Spagnoli's. He leaned on the counter and dangled one bag over the duty nurse's head until she looked up at him. It had become his ritual to bring a bag of pastries for the nurses and another bag for Ava when he visited. They looked forward to Able's visits, but more so to Mrs. Spagnoli's cannolis, cheese danishes and other delicacies.

"Aren't you just the sweetest thing," said Nurse Jean. "How can a man be so sweet and be in love with such a tyrant?"

"We have a long history," said Able. "And I'll leave it at that."

"Well, we love your visits Able," said Nurse Jean. "She's always nicer after you leave. Plus these pastries are to die for." She took a bite of a cannoli and melted into her seat with an "uuummmmm."

Able slowly opened the door to Ava's private room and jiggled the bag of pastries in the air. The smell of fresh-baked goods filled the air and gave away his presence before Able could even say hello.

"Good morning, honey bun," said Ava sweetly. "Did you bring me a honey bun today?"

Able walked over and leaned down to kiss Ava on the top of her head. The contraption she was wearing made it nearly impossible to kiss her anywhere else without hitting a bar or wire holding her together. Able pulled a warm cheese danish out of the brown paper bag and broke off a bite-size piece.

"No honey buns today," he said beginning to feed her a morsel. "But I know how you love these danishes."

Ava slowly opened her mouth and let the danish almost melt in her mouth. Able sat on the edge of her bed and had his standard blueberry muffin. They talked about her recovery some, but they mainly talked about the old days. They would reminisce about their time dating, trips to the beach, not going to the St. Margaret's dance that year and their many other exploits with Missy and James. Able would feed Ava from time to time, then hold her juice close enough so she could reach the straw without much effort. At the end of every visit Ava would apologize to Able and tears would begin to flow. Able would dab the tears with a tissue and tell her just to concentrate on getting better.

Able held Ava's hand in his and felt the warmth of her soft skin. They stared into each other's eyes for a moment and both knew it was time for him to leave. Ava needed her rest and even these short visits drained her completely. Able could tell she was getting tired. Ava's family would be coming to visit throughout the day. He enjoyed the peace and quiet of the hospital before the sun came up . . . the early mornings were Able's time with her. He leaned down and kissed Ava's hand, prince charming style, gave her a wink and headed out the door. Ava was asleep before the door clicked closed.

Able waited for the elevator across from the nurses station and wiped the tears away as they rolled down his cheeks. He just couldn't let her go. He knew that deep down she was a part of him and he was powerless to do anything about it.

Chapter Twenty-Eight

Madison, Georgia

—September 1985—

Able raced down Georgia Highway 20 heading south against an imaginary field of famous NASCAR drivers—Earnhardt, Petty and Johnson. Of course, he was in the lead and would surely cross the checkered flag victorious. The tires of his 1954 Jaguar convertible squealed as they hugged the hair-pin turn at sixty miles an hour. He shifted into fourth coming out of the turn and screamed down the straight-away pushing the needle to ninety before backing off the gas.

The pine trees that lined the highway were a dark green blur as he raced past, but their sweet smell lingered and swirled through the mahogany and leather cockpit. He downshifted when a farmer pulled onto the highway in his faded-red and rusted Massey-Ferguson tractor. He

waved Able past, so he hit the gas and swung around him quickly—in his fantasy the farmer was Junior Johnson who just blew an engine and was done for the day.

It was nearly noon on a warm and sunny Saturday without a cloud in the sky. Able was driving to the Philips 66 down the way to get some lunch, gas and some 2-stroke oil for the mower. The Philips 66 was one of those "anything-you-need-they-got" kind of places and it saved him from driving another five miles to the nearest real town.

The vintage Jaguar was his one indulgence when he started making actual money in his acting career. It was funny how things worked out, but the role brought him right back to the place he loved the most . . . the South.

It had taken him three hard years of cattle calls and embarrassing roles to get this far. He hated LA. There was more bullshit there than in all the dairy farms in Georgia. He stuck it out though, and it seemed to have paid off. The producer actually saw his Chicken Boy commercial and thought he had an indefinable, but realistic Southern charm. Gee, wonder why?

He couldn't believe his luck when his agent called about a casting call in Atlanta. His latest junker, an old red and white Chevy Blazer, had just enough get up and go to get him down to Atlanta, but he wasn't sure if it could bring him back. Luckily, it didn't have to. He was in Atlanta for a week and in that time he got the part and signed a one year deal. He went from having nearly nothing to making $20,000 per episode with a $50,000 signing bonus. Go figure.

The whole show sounded kind of stupid to him at first, but he couldn't knock the ratings. *Magnolia* was a definite rip off of *Dallas*, but set at the fictional plantation of Georgia's wealthiest family, the Buford's. They shot the outdoor scenes at a beautiful old plantation home called Heritage Hall in the town of Madison, about an hour and fifteen minutes north of Atlanta. It was said that Sherman spared the town during his march through Georgia in 1862 because his lover lived there. The inside scenes were shot at a production studio just outside of Atlanta.

Able recently bought his first house just north of town, since the show was picked up for two more seasons. The house was almost dead center between Atlanta and Madison, so it was an easy commute no matter where they were shooting.

He would call it a fixer-upper, but his friends thought it was a piece of shit money pit. It was a beautiful old farmhouse on ten acres that dated back to the mid-1800s. There were two out buildings, a big old barn and smoke house, and a small pond stocked with bass and bream. There was nothing better than coming home from a shoot and throwing a line in the water. He liked to pack a few cold Buds in his small cooler and load up his old, dinged-up canoe with some snacks and plenty of rods and lures. You know what they say about "taking the boy outta the country . . ."

The house was in good shape now that everything had been updated. The outbuildings still needed some work, as well as the landscaping, but that would come in time.

After a fun ride through the countryside in the Jag, he washed it off, put it in the barn and cinched the cover down tight. That was his baby and he planned on taking real good care of her.

He grabbed his fishing pole that hung on two rusty nails in the corner of the barn and strolled down to the nearby pond. Getting a line wet was Able's way of relaxing and allowing the stresses of life to wash away. As he worked the Texas rig slowly along a fallen tree his thoughts drifted to Ava.

After nearly six months of playing nursemaid, keeping her spirits up and helping her struggle through physical therapy, he was shocked by the abrupt ending.

"I need you to give me some space, Able," Ava told him after an AA meeting. "I really appreciate your support, but you need to take your life back, too."

Life is a funny thing. Just a few days after that conversation Able received the call about the show. His life became a whirlwind of activity and he did as she requested and took his life back.

His character on *Magnolia* was Brandon Charles Buford, III. He was not sure what it was about Southerners and their names, but that name was as realistic as it got. Of course, his parents on the show called him the full, Brandon Charles. His friends just called him BC. He was the sweet, dutiful son who was in line to take over the family fortune. His older, ruthless brother was passed over as head of the company for his many indiscretions in the past. He would do anything to regain control of their fortune, even blackmail his younger brother. Sound familiar?

Able swung the string of bass on the old work table in the outbuilding. He laid out two nice-sized bass side by side, then slid his filet knife out of the leather holster on his belt. He palmed the sharpening stone in his left hand and quickly ran the knife blade back and forth with his right. He ran his thumb along the blade's edge to ensure a clean cut.

The four filets were about the size of his palm and would be a good meal for one grown man. Hopefully, he thought, the smaller bass he released would be eating size by next fall.

The skillet hissed loudly when the pat of butter hit the pan. Able swirled it around to cover the entire surface, then dipped the filet in bread crumbs before dropping it into the pan of melted butter. Just a few minutes per side, then a little fresh lemon juice for extra flavor. The oven dinged that the cornbread was ready. He checked the

rice, which was perfect, then loaded up a plate. There was nothing better than fresh bass, wild rice and cornbread. Not bad for a bachelor with a limited culinary repertoire.

He sat down on a rickety ladder-back chair at the old farm table that he bought at an estate sale months ago. He leaned back on two legs and thumbed through the day's newspaper. He had only taken a few bites of the delicious bass when the phone rang.

He answered on the third ring to an unfamiliar voice on the other end.

"Mr. Curran," said the baritone male voice. "You don't know me, but I'm Doctor Harrell calling from Charleston, South Carolina."

"What can I do for you, doctor?" Able asked, a bit puzzled.

"A huge favor, actually. Well, not as much for me, but for an old friend of yours who's a patient of mine. I'm sure you remember Ava Dubose," said Doctor Harrell.

"Of course," Able said. "How's she doing?"

"Well, she's been coming to me for the past few months since leaving the hospital and your name has come up in practically every session," he said sounding a bit surprised. "Ava has agreed that you should come in and join us for a session, if it's not too inconvenient."

Chapter 28

"You realize, doctor, that I live in Atlanta—a good four hours from Charleston?"

"I know it's asking a lot, Mr. Curran, but I really think it could be helpful. I'm getting one side of Ava's story here and you must know how convincing she can be? I think there's more to what she's telling me and I really need another perspective."

Able laughed and shook his head. At least this doctor was sharp enough to see what was going on. In the past, Ava's doctors believed whatever she said. They assumed that through all the tears and repentance came the truth. They based her drinking and drugging on less-than-attentive parents and a family history of addiction. Each time she fell off the wagon, it was a cry for help—or so they thought.

"I can take off work this Friday, if that works," Able said.

"That's just fine," said the doctor, a bit relieved. "I have an appointment with Ava at two o'clock."

The doctor gave Able directions to his office in a little strip mall on the outskirts of Charleston on the Savannah Highway "just past the Krispy Kreme." He told Able that Ava knew he would be coming, but that she wasn't aware that he would be used as truth serum for her stories.

It was Monday morning and he couldn't wait until Friday to see her again.

Able inspected himself in the mirror of a convenience store bathroom a few blocks from Dr. Harrell's office. He stopped to buy a pack of gum and to make sure he looked good before seeing Ava again after all this time. He questioned his decision to stop at this establishment as his nostrils filled with the stench of dried urine the moment he entered the bathroom. There was disgustingly graphic graffiti on the walls and general filth all around. The trash can was over flowing with balled up paper towels and the floor was covered in a film of grey gunk. A condom dispenser hung on one wall offering a selection of fruity colors, a French Tickler and one labeled King Dong. Able washed his hands then reached for a paper towel to find the dispenser empty. He flicked the water off his hands then patted them on the thighs of his pants to dry them off. He pulled the door handle open with one pinky finger and slipped through the door quickly to avoid any jumping germs. He purchased a pack of mint gum to ensure fresh breath, then drove the final few blocks to the doctor's office.

The strip mall had such a strange grouping of businesses that Able did a double-take to make sure he was in the right place. There were five store fronts that did not complement each other at all . . . a laundry mat, a Chinese Restaurant, Dr. Harrell's office, a video poker parlor and a Bail Bondsman. Able looked over at the Krispy Kreme store, then back at the strange strip mall, then down at his hand written directions. The lettering on the middle door was "Dr. Stanley Harrell, MD, Psychologist."

"Hmm," Able thought. "I guess this is the right place."

He pushed his way through the doorway and into a small reception area. A bell dinged as he entered. There was a reception desk, but no receptionist, no phone and no waiting area chairs. There were a few framed posters on the walls of various countries with their iconic images . . . France with the Eiffel Tower, England with Big Ben, Spain with a bullfighter. Able questioned the directions and nearly started to leave.

"Hello, Mr. Curran, I presume," said Dr. Harrell as he popped out from behind the reception wall.

"Yes, Docter Harrell?" questioned Able.

Doctor Harrell noticed the puzzled look on Able's face and quickly started explaining.

"I'm sorry, I'm sorry," he began. "I should have mentioned this used to be a travel agency and I just haven't had the time to decorate, or hire a receptionist . . . or buy any furniture." He seemed to realize his shortcomings as an independent businessman as he reeled off what he hadn't yet done.

"Well, let's step in here where I do actually have an office," he said with a light chuckle and directed Able through the doorway. "Ava is waiting for us."

Able's hands got clammy and his throat tightened. He pushed the door fully open and took a few steps into a large office space. He stopped when he saw Ava sitting in a leather office chair, legs crossed and staring at him. She was wearing a jean skirt cut to mid-thigh, a loose-fitting white cotton sweater with a scoop neck and strappy turquoise pumps. Around her neck was a chunky turquoise necklace with matching dangling earrings. Her hair had grown out since he last saw her and now hung well past her shoulders. A simple black hair band kept it neat and stylish.

Ava stood up slowly and placed her hands on her hips.

"Are you gonna just stand there looking stupid," she said with a grin. "Or are you gonna stroll your ass over here and give me a hug?" She reached her arms out and smiled her perfect smile.

Able double-timed it across the room and threw his arms around Ava like her past digressions had never happened. They hugged each other tightly and did not speak. They melted into each other just like they had years before.

"OK, OK," said Dr. Harrell after several minutes. "You're on the clock, you know, so let's everyone have a seat and talk about things."

Ava and Able released their grip on one another and settled into the two leather chairs opposite the doctor's desk. Ava reached over and held Able's hand. She smiled for a moment staring into his eyes, remembering. Then without warning she broke down crying, burying her face in her hands. Able leapt from his chair and kneeled down in front of her, consoling her. He reached around to hug her neck and pulled her close.

"Shhh, shhh, it's all right," he whispered in her ear. "It's gonna be all right, Ava."

"Fuck!" she shouted after a few moments and she sat up straight. "What the fuck is wrong with me? I don't do this shit . . . I don't cry like this . . . fuck!" She wiped the tears from under her eyes making sure to keep her mascara neat through it all. She fanned her face with both hands to dry the tears rolling down her cheeks.

The doctor motioned for Able to take his seat.

"I think this is fabulous, Ava," said Doctor Harrell finally. "I haven't seen you emit this kind of emotion in six months. I think Mr. Curran here has struck a nerve, don't you?"

"Shut the fuck up, Stanley," Ava barked. "You've been waiting for a breakthrough. Well, here's your fucking breakthrough. Are you happy! Fucking quack."

Dr. Harrell laughed loudly and slapped at his desk. He smiled at Able and shook his head in wonderment. Able looked back at the doctor with a puzzled look.

"Oh, Mr. Curran, don't be alarmed," he said still chuckling. "Ava calls me a quack on a regular basis. I know she really values my opinion and the quack comments are only a byproduct of her processing her feelings. When she calls me a quack I know that we are getting somewhere. This is fabulous, just fabulous!"

"Well, doctor," said Able rather sheepishly. "Where do we go from here? Where do we start?"

"At the beginning, my good man," said Doctor Harrell enthusiastically. "We start at the beginning."

Ava glanced at Able. She looked tired, he thought. Tired, but beautiful. They locked eyes for what seemed like minutes and studied each other closely. Finally, Ava nodded at Able. A nod that said go, start, tell our story . . . from the beginning.

Able turned to the doctor. "Well," he said as he took a deep breath. "Well, it all started at a fraternity party almost five years ago."

Chapter Twenty-Nine

Atlanta, Georgia

—June 1986—

The front door was ajar, so Able pushed his way in with a hard knock and a "you hoo" as he stepped into the foyer. There was no answer, but he could hear the low rumble of conversations coming from the back of the house. Able walked through the well-appointed living room with a baby grand piano in one corner and lovely art work on every wall. He continued through the study with dark wooden bookshelves, a well-worn leather sofa with needle point throw pillows with a "G" and bulldog pattern. The homeowner was a University of Georgia alumni and his pride showed through the photos of his football playing days that adorned the walls in the room. A photo of Coach Vince Dooley with the inscription, "To Al, the toughest son of a bitch I know, Coach Dooley," hung prominently over the doorway as one entered the kitchen.

"Able, darlin', you made it," called Susan Phillips, wife of the tough son of a bitch. "Where have you been, darlin', you're an hour late. We're getting ready to sit down to eat so grab a drink. The bar's on the patio."

"I'm sorry, Susan," said Able. "But the drive in from Madison is 45 minutes and Friday night traffic in Atlanta is a bear." He offered her a bottle of wine as his hostess gift. "Forgive me?"

"Oh darlin', you are always forgiven," she said then kissed him on the cheek. "Oh, I love this Pinot, thank you, darlin'. Come on now, outside, outside. I want you to meet someone."

Susan pushed Able out the kitchen door that lead to the large brick patio adjacent to a small pool behind the house. Al and Susan Phillips got married right out of college and quickly had a few children. Al was an All American linebacker at Georgia and played pro ball for the Atlanta Falcons for two years before having his right knee folded back the wrong way in a game against the Cowboys. He became a commercial developer and was now a big player in transforming the Atlanta skyline. Susan was a cheerleader and fell in love with Al from the sidelines. She went on to get her masters in engineering at Georgia Tech and was now president of Peachtree Engineering. She and Al were a power couple and movers and shakers in Atlanta.

They bought the brick Georgian house with football money and renovated it to their liking, including the pool and pool house before the injury. Al and Susan were one of those disgustingly wonderful, loving and successful couples.

"Wait, wait, wait," said Able pulling away from Susan. "Let me grab a drink then you can introduce me around to everyone."

"Ok, darlin'," said Susan pointing to the other side of the pool. "But meet me over there in a few minutes. I have someone special for you to meet."

Able nodded hello to several guests as he made his way to the bar. He grabbed a tall glass and filled it with ice. He uncapped the waxy red top of a bottle of Makers Mark and tipped it for a nice pour. He finished it off with a splash of ginger ale then swirled the drink with his finger.

"You know that's disgusting, don't you?" said a sweet, southern voice. "They've got stirring sticks right there."

"My finger, my drink," said Able looking to his right and smiling. Then he licked the dripping liquid off his finger. "Yum! Care for one?" he asked.

"Sure," she said. "I love a good B&G, but hold the finger."

Able made her the drink and stared at her intently as he stirred it with his index finger before offering her the drink, finger still stirring. She took his hand and lifted his finger out of her drink, then pulled it up to her mouth and sucked off the excess liquid. Able's eyes widened at the unexpected turn of events.

"Mmm," she purred. "That does give it a certain Old Spice finish, now doesn't it."

"Now that you've sucked on my finger I should probably introduce myself," said Able wiping his hand on his pant leg then extending it to shake. "I'm Able Curran."

"So, you're Able," she said a bit surprised. "Oh no, now I'm really embarrassed," she said as she covered her eyes and turned away for a moment. "I'm June Sessoms, uh, Susan's friend. I think she may have mentioned me."

"No, no," said Able grabbing her shoulders, "don't be embarrassed. We're just goofing around. Really, don't be embarrassed. Really, it's fine."

Just then Susan bounded up to break the awkward moment. "Hey, y'all finally met," she said excitedly. "I told you he was a cutie pie, didn't I, June? You all look so good together . . . just the perfect couple. Yeeaahh!" Susan clapped her hands quickly like she was speed praying.

Susan was a bit shocked when she heard the story of sucking bourbon off fingers, but she thought it made for a great "meet cute" that they could tell their children.

June and Able were not so sure it was a story that needed to be repeated. They did sit together at dinner and spoke only to each other. The drone of conversation all around them was evidence that no one cared they were in their own little world.

Able learned that June was an advertising executive working for a regional magazine. She was a University of Virginia graduate who grew up in Charleston and had lived in Atlanta for the past five years. Her goal was to move back to Charleston someday and raise kids by the water. June was intrigued by Able's acting career and she didn't care he was a college dropout.

They looked up and noticed everyone else had left or were back on the patio for a night cap. They were the only ones still at the table. It was well past midnight and Able had to pry himself away since he had a long drive home.

"When can I see you again," Able said to June as they held hands in the front yard. "I've got some time later this week if you want to have dinner."

"My week is really slammed," said June dejectedly. "I'm in New York on Tuesday, then Miami on Wednesday and back here on Friday. How's your weekend? I could do Saturday."

"Saturday it is then," said Able with a smile. "Do you want to come out to my place in Madison? It's a beautiful old house. I can grill some steaks and we can have bourbons by the pond."

"That sounds lovely," said June. "Call me this week and give me the address and directions." She handed Able her business card, then leaned in to kiss him on the cheek. "It was great meeting you Able," she said with a smile.

Able climbed into his old Jaguar and admired June's business card by the dash light. "June Sessoms, Regional Advertising Director," he said out loud. "So this is what a real woman is like . . . beautiful, smart, successful and she likes to laugh. I could get used to this." Able looked up at June waiting at the front stoop and waved goodbye.

The pine trees zipped by in a blur as Able raced down highway 20 back to Madison. His mind was clear with no other thought than the image of June. Her long brown hair waving in the breeze, the twinkle in her emerald green eyes and her full on laugh at one of Able's stupid jokes. He turned up the volume on the radio as the drone of the engine filled his ears. "This is the Day" by The The blared out through the speakers . . . "This is the day your life will surely change, this is the day when things fall into place . . ."

Able laughed to himself at the irony, then just smiled and let the lyrics pump out loudly as he drummed the steering wheel. He smiled all the way home with thoughts of June swirling through his head.

Chapter Thirty

Charleston, South Carolina

—April 1988—

A black limousine stopped in front of Ava's condo in her quaint neighborhood in Mount Pleasant and waited. After a few minutes, the red front door to her condo opened and Ava appeared under the lamplight. She wore a pale yellow strapless dress that was cut just below her knees and hugged her curves nicely. Her hair was pulled back and held in place with a lovely pearl beret. She wore white gloves that stopped just above her wrists and carried a small white purse that contained the essentials . . . lipstick, mascara and a few credit cards. White three-inch pumps with a yellow bow on the toe completed her stunning ensemble.

The door to the limousine opened as Ava approached. She gracefully stepped in and settled in the plush leather seat. A Martini with two olives was handed to her almost immediately.

"Can't you at least get out of the fucking car and come to my door?" Ava said in a disgusted tone. "I feel like a Goddamn hooker when you treat me like this, William."

William Randolph Holt was a prominent Charleston businessman and the new Republican nominee for the US Senate from South Carolina. He was fifty-five years old, handsome and happily married with two adoring children. Well, at least that's what the newspaper and television stations reported on a daily basis.

Ava and William met at a fundraiser months earlier at the home of the president of Palmetto Shipping International, George Hunt's family business. George was asked to attend and to bring a date, so naturally he called Ava. At the time, Ava was on the wagon and not interested in George's repeated request to party in the guest bathroom. So, he befriended another young woman who was interested. After snorting the blow George had on hand, they decided to walk the four blocks to his house to party some more before heading out on the town. George didn't have the decency to say goodbye to Ava, he was rarely decent, but he knew Ava would be fine.

William found Ava standing out on the veranda by herself, sipping a Shirley Temple, and enjoying the soft summer breeze coming off the water. She quickly turned around when he approached.

"I didn't mean to startle you," he said coolly. "It's a beautiful night."

"You didn't and yes, it is," said Ava staring up at him.

"I'm William Randolph Holt," he said rather politician-like and extended his hand to greet her.

"I think it's safe to say that almost everyone in South Carolina knows who you are, don't you?" Ava said without shaking his hand. "If not, then it's time to fire your campaign manager."

"Well, I was really just attempting a formal introduction so I could learn your name," he answered calmly. "I'm not always looking for votes, you know."

Ava stared at him for a good thirty seconds before reacting. "Ava Gardner Dubose, at your service Mr. Holt. Now, is that what you wanted or do you want something else?" she asked.

"Please, call me William," he said with a grin. "May I get you another, ah, what are you drinking?"

"No, thank you," she said. "I can't drink another Shirley Temple or I'll start tap dancing uncontrollably." She noticed his puzzled look and continued. "Raging alcoholic," she said matter-of-factly. "I could tell you the whole history, but it's really all the same story with a different ending each time . . . waking up in a strange place and usually with someone I didn't remember meeting."

"I'm sorry to hear that," said William. "I'm glad you're clean and sober now."

"Well," said Ava. "It never seems to last very long, so you may be in for a treat one of these days. That is, if I ever see you again."

That was two months ago and they had seen each other again and again since that first meeting. That night, William had his chauffeur take Ava home, get her phone number and find out about her interest in joining him for a low-key rendezvous. They had met discretely one night each week since then.

The chauffeur pushed a buttom on the console and the privacy window closed tightly. The Bee Gees' "How deep is your love" oozed faintly out of the rear speakers as the long, back car with smokey black windows pulled away slowly from the curb.

"I'm sorry, darling, but you know I can't be seen walking to your door to pick you up," he said it like he actually cared. "We've got to keep a low profile."

He leaned over and kissed her on the neck, then on the cheek, then on the mouth. They kissed passionately for a minute as the limo slowly cruised down Palmetto Way and began their one-hour mobile date.

"My God, you are so beautiful," he said running his hand across her body.

"Wait, wait, wait," said Ava. "You're going to mess up my outfit before we even get over the bridge. I want a bump first anyway; do you have it?"

William could barely contain himself. Even strong men are weaker than the weakest woman when sex is anywhere in sight. History will continually repeat itself as long as men fall prey to their animal instincts of uncontrollable sexual desire in the presence of a strong, sexy and smart woman. Ava had the next US Senator from South Carolina wrapped around her cocaine-stained pinky and there wasn't a damn thing he could do about it.

William reached into his coat pocket and pulled out a five-ounce bag of cocaine, her weekly allotment. He handed it to Ava who opened it, scooped up a small amount with her pinky nail and snorted it quickly into her right nostril. She could tell it was good stuff. She scooped another hit and snorted it with the other nostril. She felt a warm, tingling sensation fill her body. She had already forgotten about William not picking her up at the door.

They drank champagne and Ava took the occasional bump as they rode through Charleston and over bridges that spanned the salt marsh between the various island towns. This was the standard routine of their weekly dates since they could not afford to be seen in public. They munched on a variety of light hors-d'oeuvres and

nibbled on each other. Finally, before William was about to explode Ava allowed him to explore her body. She slid out of her dress to reveal a sexy, intricately laced bra and matching underpants. She made William admire her for a few minutes before she unleashed herself to him. They made love in the back of the limousine until they both collapsed in blissful exhaustion.

Ava took another bump and asked William to make love to her again.

"Let me rest for a while," he said, still breathing heavily. "I need about thirty minutes, baby, then we'll go again."

Ava didn't feel like waiting. She pushed William back on the leather seat and scooped up a pinky nail full of cocaine. She leaned over and sprinkled cocaine on the tip of William's penis and began to rub it in. William tried to stop her, but it was too late. He was nearly ready and after a few more minutes Ava climbed on top of him and moved her hips slowly. Ava moaned with passion and William took the credit for making her feel so good. However, the cocaine didn't just bring him back, but it heightened her arousal too. A junkie will take it any way they can get it.

It was nearly 1:00 a.m. when the limo stopped in front of Ava's condo. Both of them were now dressed and resting against each other. The speaker in the back of the limo crackled on, "Sir, we're here."

“That was incredible,” he said. “I’ve never tried that before.”

“Stick with me baby and you’ll say that a few more times before we’re done,” said Ava in her sexiest voice. She leaned over and kissed William, then wiped the lipstick off his mouth. “See you next week, sugar daddy.”

William grabbed her arm to keep her from leaving. She turned and looked at him.

“I think I love you, Ava,” he said looking deep into her eyes.

“I know,” she answered with a smile. She climbed out of the limo, blew him a kiss and walked to her front door without looking back.

Chapter Thirty-One

Charleston, South Carolina

—February 1994—

Regardless of its location, Low Country Treatment Center in Summerville, South Carolina was a cold and sterile place. The white tile floors with white walls and white ceilings would confuse anyone if it were not for the crisp red, blue and green lines that directed patients through the facility. The occasional print on the wall and fake plants didn't do much to brighten-up the place. It smelled like rubbing alcohol, and occasionally the pungent odor of vomit wafted through the hallway. Meeting rooms for group therapy or private sessions were on each hall and screams, cries for help and whimpers oozed under the doorways to the ears of passers-by. It was hard to imagine anyone could get used to those surroundings, but they did.

Ava's stay in rehab this time was made a bit easier because of Demarcus Johnson, an orderly on the night shift at LCTC. Demarcus received his degree from a local community college as a nurse technician about five years ago. He had been a model employee for the first four years; he even received the "Employee of the Year" in 1992, but he grew tired of the paltry raises and his current $12.25 an hour rate. Demarcus started dealing a variety of prescription and street drugs to his captive audience, who would pay any price to not feel what they were supposed to feel.

The going rate was twenty dollars per pill for Vicodin, Percocet or Zoloft and fifty dollars for a key hit of coke. He didn't deal in marijuana or anything requiring needles, as they were too easily detectable. Demarcus did well for himself with a strong cash business and he even made trades for watches, jewelry, shoes or anything else that he could sell or use himself. It was never a problem unloading the traded items and he usually sold things to close friends or relatives. Demarcus was pocketing an extra $500 a week and did well enough in just the first few months to upgrade from a Honda Civic to a brand new Cadillac Seville. He could be convinced to trade his goods for sex too, but he was very particular about whom to extend that type of credit. Ava had carte blanche in that regard and used it regularly once her cash and jewels were gone. The one item she would not part with was the cameo. She would open the locket each night before bedtime and kiss the photograph of her Grande.

"God, please make me better," she would pray. "Make me stop wanting the pills and cocaine and let me have a regular life. And please allow my Grande to forgive me for all the bad things I have done. Amen."

Her day of freedom finally arrived and Ava walked down the corridor towards reception to check out of a rehab center for the eighth time in her thirty-two years on this earth and no visit had given her more than a year of sobriety. Her parents were coming to pick her up—again—and they were growing tired of the ritual.

"Well, Ms. Ava," said Cindy Weaver, the always friendly receptionist. "You leaving us today, honey?" Cindy was younger than Ava, but she was one of those Southern girls who called everyone honey. She had bright red hair that she styled in a 1970s throwback bun and wore a cardigan over her nurse whites, as she tended to get chilly. Her relentless happiness drove most people up the wall, including Ava.

"Shor'is, Ms. Cindy, honey," Ava said being sarcastically Southern. Ava leaned over to sign the discharge papers with a quick flick of her wrist. "I've been dreaming of this day for four fucking months. Thank God I'm free."

"You be good out there, honey," said Ms. Cindy, taking the paperwork and adjusting her glasses. "We don't want to see you back here again. You be strong now, Ms. Ava, you hear!"

Ava wiped her mouth with the back of her hand, then picked up the pack of Marlboro Lights off the dashboard, tapped out a cigarette and lit it. She sucked hard and inhaled until her lungs filled with smoke. She exhaled through her nose and let out a long sigh.

"Let's go, Goddammit," she said as tiny clouds of smoke puffed out of her mouth with each word. "A deal's a deal. Now get me the fuck outta here!"

"You just hold yer horses there, girlie," said the stranger in a thick Southern drawl. "I can't very well drive with my britches 'round my ankles now, can I?" He struggled to put himself back together and buckle up. He stared at Ava for a moment, then reached over and grabbed her chest. She slapped his hand away and glared at him for only a second, which was all it took.

"All right, all right," he said, getting the clue. "Serves me right for gettin' greedy. Charleston, here we come."

The stranger eased the truck into first gear . . . three on the tree . . . and they drove along Interstate 26 in relative silence. The only sound was country music playing softly through the blown speakers and the constant rattle of the ratty, well-worn green, early 70s Ford pick-up truck.

Ava had walked out of the rehab center less than an hour before and headed straight for the interstate. She waited on the on-ramp in an ivory color silk blouse, black dress pants and three inch black pumps. Her mother made her put on something "respectable" before entering rehab this time. The clothes had hung neatly in her closet since the day she checked in. It certainly was not your typical hitch hiker attire, but it surely captured the driver's attention.

She didn't care who picked her up or how she got there. She just wanted a fix and was willing to do anything to get there. The stranger stopped after Ava had her thumb in the air for only a few minutes.

"Where you headed, ma'am?" he said with a kind Southern drawl. "I'm happy to hep if I ken." He was caught off guard by her suggested deal, but figured this must be his lucky day.

"Take me to Charleston and I'll make you a happy man," she said very matter of factly. It was her first and only offer. The stranger knew what she meant and took it. It was not Ava's finest hour, but she had done worse things before. An addict looking for a fix will do just about anything to make it happen and Ava was a full-tilt addict.

The stranger was in his early fifties, but easily looked sixty. He obviously worked outside as his skin was wrinkled and dark. The black under his fingernails gave away that his days were filled with manual labor. He wore filthy jeans that were covered in oil and mud stains, but his red plaid Dickies snap button work shirt was relatively clean. A spare pack of Marlboro Lights lay nestled in his shirt pocket for future use. His teeth and fingers were dank with a golden hue . . . evidence that he'd been smoking for years. The stranger knew he was lucky to have a girl of Ava's quality in his lap and he relished the moment. A twenty-mile detour was a small price to pay for such pleasure.

"Take this exit, then go left," said Ava, as she scooted to the edge of the well-worn bucket seat. She was anxious and took another long pull off the cigarette. She tried to push the memory of her recent exchange from her mind. Ava's mind raced with a jumble of thoughts, good and bad, but the bad were winning. Small beads of sweat formed on her forehead and glistened in the afternoon light. Her hands began to tremble uncontrollably. She wiped her brow, then sat back and folded her arms into her body to hold on tight.

"Whatever you need," said the stranger noticing Ava's internal torment. "You need it bad, don't you girlie."

"Shut the fuck up and drive," Ava yelled as she began to rock back and forth. Her body could sense it was close and the want for a fix was unbearable. Suddenly, Ava stopped the rocking, slapped the dashboard and pointed.

"Here, here," she screamed. "Turn right on Huger, then left on Nassau! Left, you idiot, left!"

The stranger downshifted quickly, grinding the stick into second gear. The old truck tires squealed against the rutted pavement of the neglected streets. Obviously, this area was not a priority for the DOT. Immediately the tone of the drive turned dark and dreary with boarded-up homes and abandoned cars on all sides. Trash was strewn about the street and sidewalk. "Keep out" and "No Trespassing" signs were spray painted on many of the row houses. The thumping base of a rap song coming from an unidentified source overwhelmed the soft country ballad playing on the truck's radio. Every pair of eyes on the sidewalk watched the truck as it slowly continued down the street.

Nassau Street was well known by all in town—from the Charleston elite to the gutter rats—as the place to service any addiction, or casual hobby. The college kids went there for their semester's supply of weed, the blue bloods went there for their powder and the hardcore junkies went there for the hardcore fix of crack or heroin. Any car that came through this neighborhood was one of three things—a customer, a cop or a new recruit looking to pop a cap in rival colors. Several sidewalk onlookers slid their hand into jacket pockets or reached around to the waistband of their baggy pants, wherever they kept their piece, just in case any trouble went down.

"Stop here," said Ava slapping at the dashboard. "Stop!"

"Are you sure about this, girlie?" the stranger said a bit hesitant. "I don't know if that's the best idea. They will eat you alive."

Ava wasn't in the mood to discuss the situation. She pulled back on the door handle and opened the door slightly, then looked at the stranger. He knew she was serious and hit the brakes, stopping in the middle of the narrow street. Ava jumped out of the truck without even so much as a "thanks for the lift" and without her pocket book or suitcase. She got to the sidewalk and looked up and down the street. Several young men adorned in replica NBA jerseys, gold chains and other bling approached the truck as the stranger was about to call out for Ava to fetch her belongings. The stranger thought better of it, threw the stick shift into first gear, and stomped on the gas.

He turned right onto Mary Street and drove one block south to Meeting Street and stopped. In that one block he went from scared for his life to tapping out a soothing cigarette. The cigarette dangled from his chapped and cracked lips as he reached down to the floorboard to grab Ava's bags. He pulled a few dollars out of her purse and a pair of white cotton underpants out of her bag. He pressed the underpants against his face and breathed in deeply. They smelled clean and fresh with just a hint of Ava's perfume. The stranger paused for a moment to remember Ava's gift to him and smiled at the recollection.

He reached over and opened the passenger door, about to throw the duffle bag onto the sidewalk. He thought the better of it for a second then closed the passenger door and pulled the purse tight to his side. She's too fucked up to miss this stuff, he thought. The old truck started up with a loud bang from the muffler, then a plume of gray smoke. The stranger headed back to the highway and on with his day. The boys at the shop would never believe him, but he would tell the story anyway.

Chapter Thirty-Two

Charleston, South Carolina

—February 1994—

Able's cell phone rang just as he was about to step into the shower after a long, meditative run. It was going on 4:00 p.m. and his wife and daughter Maggie would be arriving soon from school. He figured by the time he showered, shaved and threw something on that they would be home and ready for some family time. It would be another evening of rainbow drawings and hop scotch with sidewalk chalk until bedtime, then Daddy stories for Maggie, and bad television with June, so the distraction of a phone call didn't bother him too much. He picked up the phone off the vanity and studied the number for a moment. The number was vaguely familiar, but he just couldn't place it.

"Able Curran," he said rather business-like, just in case.

"Able, honey," said a soft Southern voice. "It's Margot Dubose. I'm sorry to disturb you."

"No, no, not at all," he said, a bit stunned. "I haven't spoken to you in years, Mrs. Dubose. Is something wrong?"

Ava's mother had only called Able a few times in the fifteen or so years that he knew her, so something had to be wrong. His stomach tightened and his heart pounded out of control as he anticipated the worst. He always had a fear of receiving the call that Ava was found dead in a ditch somewhere and just hoped it would never come. Everyone close to Ava had the same fear.

"Well, we hope not," she said. "I'm praying that you've heard from Ava today; have you?"

"No, ma'am," he said. "I haven't spoken to Ava since I went up there for a therapy session years ago. What's going on?"

"Oh my God," she said in a trembling voice. "Oh my God. Where's my baby? Where's my baby girl?"

"Mrs. Dubose," Able said anxiously. "Tell me what's going on. Please!"

There was a loud wail and deep soulful sobs filtered in through the phone. A moment later, Mr. Dubose came on the line and began to fill Able in on the events of the day. When they went to the treatment center to pick up

Ava after four months of treatment—she wasn't there. In the past, Ava was admitted by a doctor or by her parents and was required to be checked out by one or the other. This time, however, she admitted herself, so she was able to sign herself out as well. She called her parents the day before her release and told them to pick her up at 2:00 p.m. She was released at noon.

"We've called everyone who she may have gotten in touch with, Able," he said in his kind, fatherly way. "You're our last hope."

"Mr. Dubose, if she's looking to use again, then I'm certainly the last person she would call," he said trying to think of all the options. "If she lied to you about the pick-up time, then she's not looking for a friend—she's got to be on the street looking for a fix."

"She's been out of treatment for four Goddamn hours," he said, raising his voice to Able for the first time ever. "She can't be looking for a fix already. Goddammit, she just got out of treatment!"

Able gave them a few other numbers to call and wished them luck. They thanked him for his help throughout the years and said they would call if they had any news.

Able took a quick shower, shaved, got dressed, then headed over the bridge to Charleston. Along the way he called June to tell her the news and beg forgiveness.

"This sounds really bad honey," Able said to his understanding wife. "For her to lie about the pick up time and now be missing means she has fallen off the wagon again and really hard this time."

They spoke for a while longer about how long he would be gone, when would he be back home and what June should tell Maggie.

"Tell her I am helping a friend," he suggested. Then they exchanged I love you's and said goodnight.

Able called the Charleston Police next, who were of little help. Ava had only been missing for five hours now and that didn't meet with their twenty-four hour minimum.

"Officer, please," Able said as calmly as possible. "I'm not asking you to put out an APB, just make your beat cops aware of what's going on, a brief description, something."

"She's probably with friends and just hasn't called in," said the officer on the phone. "We can't divert manpower for every crack whore that goes missing." He paused. "I'm sorry 'bout that, it's been a long day. Look, give us a call tomorrow if she still hasn't turned up and we'll see what we can do."

A lot could happen over the next sixteen hours and Able just couldn't wait for the authorities to put this "crack whore" on their to-do list. He lived in the suburbs of

Charleston and had been into the city plenty of times over the years and knew what neighborhoods to avoid. This trip would include a tour of all of those neighborhoods where he dared not go before.

Chapter Thirty-Three

Nassau Street: Charleston, South Carolina

"Hey, mama," said a thirty-something black man with short, one-inch high baby dreadlocks. "You too fine to be alone in my 'hood. You lost, or you just want some big, black love?" He stepped closer, reached out and grabbed Ava behind the neck. "I don't think you're lost, bitch."

"I need to find Two Peace," said Ava very matter-of-factly.

"Damn, bitch," he said with a laugh. "You must be all fucked up if you lookin' for Two Peace. He deals in that serious shit. Well, bitch, you know that kind of information ain't free, don't cha. What you gonna give Ray Ray for the privilege?"

He moved his hand from behind her neck and slid it down the nape of her neck to her chest. He lifted the cameo from between her cleavage and admired it. He placed the cameo back to her skin gently, then palmed her left breast with his large, ringed right hand. Ava stood motionless. His hand moved from breast to breast, then down to her stomach and finally settled between her legs.

"I guess you need it pretty bad," he said palming her crotch. "You gonna give Ray Ray whatever he wants, ain't cha, bitch? Damn, you junkies are fucked up." He laughed loudly and looked around to the others who were watching for his next move. They called out terrible suggestions, but Ava stood her ground. "I'll tell you what I want, bitch," he said pressing his hand between her legs even harder now. "I'll take this." He let go of her crotch and took hold of the cameo around Ava's neck. He quickly jerked the gold chain, then stood there admiring his latest acquisition. He pushed on the side latch and the cameo opened up to reveal a photograph of Grande.

"Oh, hell yeah," he said all excited. "Mama gonna love this for Christmas." He pulled out the photo of Grande and it dropped to the ground. He clicked the lid back shut and stuffed the cameo and chain in his front pocket.

Ava had remained standing with not so much as a flinch for the past few minutes. The only motion now detectable was a single tear that welled up in her eye and slowly ran down her cheek. "I'm sorry, Grande," she said to herself. It was the first time she had felt any real human emotion in months.

Ray Ray escorted Ava several blocks down Nassau Street to an old, dilapidated row house that had to be over a hundred years old. There were ornately scrolled cornices at the roof and beautiful wood work that trimmed the windows and front door. Potato chip sized pink paint flakes curled up on most every board just waiting for wind or rain to finish it off. The rusted wrought iron gate was nothing more than a trellis for weeds. Trash and debris littered the sidewalk and shards of glass from broken windows crackled under foot with each step. The lower windows were boarded up with plywood and the upstairs windows had sheets or towels hung to keep out the sunlight. Ray Ray greeted a young black man who sat on the front stoop.

"Two Peace," said Ray Ray as he shook the man's hand. The man simply gestured with a nod of his head indicating to go up, then went back to his own contemplation.

The old door creaked loudly as they entered the house. There was more litter inside than out and a stale, pungent funk filled the air. Blankets and clothes were strewn about on the floor, along with beer cans and whisky bottles. They passed several doors that were closed with strange moans and shrieks coming from inside. The one door that was open revealed a trashed bedroom with mattresses on the floor. A solitary figure sat in a tattered chair in the corner of the room. He was silhouetted against the bit of sunlight that forced its way into the room as white smoke wafted up around him.

They made their way to the second floor up the front staircase that creaked with the slightest movement. The old, rounded handrail was hand carved with a lovely scrolled newel post with several of the delicately carved balusters missing every few feet. The railing was still relatively sturdy given its age and history of supporting the patrons of this place over the years. The temperature increased as they reached the second floor, which intensified the musty funk. The smell of old house mixed with dried urine, vomit and junkie stench was nearly unbearable.

"Yo, Two Peace!" shouted Ray Ray to the first closed doors. "I got you a present that I think you gonna like, brother! Yo, Two Peace!"

The furthest door on the right creaked open a few inches, then closed. The clang of a door chain echoed through the hall and the door opened again. There were no words spoken, but Ava made her way to the doorway and slipped inside. The door closed with a bang and the door chain rattled against the wood as it was locked again.

"All right now," shouted Ray Ray at the closed door. "I'll be seeing y'all later. You remember who's bringing you fine white bitches now, all right Two Peace. It's your boy,

Ray Ray looking out for ya. All right, now. I'm out!" Ray Ray ran down the stairs and out the front door. He squinted at the sunlight and breathed in the fresh air, then made his way back to his corner.

Two Peace turned around to greet Ava. "Peace, baby, peace," he said in his deep, soft voice. "I haven't seen you in awhile. I thought you went clean on me."

"I've been inside for the past four months," said Ava rubbing her arms to keep warm even though it was pushing eighty degrees inside. "You know people like us can't stay clean for long. So, can you help me out?"

Two Peace went to the table and opened up an old Dutch Masters cigar box. He pulled out a syringe and placed it on the table, then a long piece of rubber and, finally a small vile of liquid. Ava walked over quickly and reached for the syringe, but Two Peace grabbed her by the wrist.

"What do you think you're doing, bitch?" he said in a deep, guttural voice. "You know you don't play before you pay." He held out his other hand, but Ava just looked up at him with desperate eyes. "Oh, I see how it is now," he said. "Well, I do take cash or trade. So, what they be trading today, baby?"

Two Peace let go of Ava's wrist and took a step back. He slowly sat back in his La-Z-Boy and got comfortable. Ava stood before him and unbuttoned her silk, cream

colored blouse. She slid it off her shoulders and it fell quietly to the floor. She unlatched her bra that connected in the front and tossed it to the side. She took a step towards Two Peace, who stopped her in her tracks.

"No, no," he said. "Keep going, bitch. I'll tell you when to stop."

Ava slowly lowered the zipper at the side of her dress pants. They fell around her ankles and she stepped out and kicked them away. She stood there in a pair of black strappy pumps and black lace panties. Two Peace made a rotating motion with his hand that could only mean one thing. Ava pulled her underpants down over her wide hips and they fell to the floor to join her pile of belongings. She stood there in all her glory—nude and shaking uncontrollably like the junkie she had become.

Two Peace unbuckled his belt and pulled his jeans and briefs down to his knees. He reached down and pulled the lever of his La-Z-Boy to set it to the full recline position. He lay back and motioned to Ava. She had been in this position before and knew just what to do.

After a good half hour, Two Peace pushed Ava to the floor when he was finished with her. She pulled herself up by the table, then reached for the syringe again. Two Peace grabbed her shoulder and spun her around quickly. He slapped her across the face and she fell to the floor.

"You don't get the shit 'til you pay in full, bitch," he yelled. "I think I need some more payment, bitch. And, it's coming outta your ass!"

Two Peace kneeled down next to Ava, who looked up slowly. His cold eyes glared back at her full of hate. He breathed heavily, nostrils flaring as sweat dripped off his face. He reared back and slapped Ava across the face again and ordered her not to look at him. He picked her up off the floor just to knock her back down again with a back handed slap to the other cheek. She could feel her face beginning to swell when Two Peace grabbed a handful of long, blonde hair and pulled her back to her feet.

"How does it feel to be a junkie and a fuckin' whore," he yelled. "Huh, bitch, how does it fuckin' feel."

He threw her across the room and she fell over a small, ratty wooden chair and into the corner with a crash. She lay there with her arms covering her head in case there was another blow. Two Peace picked up the small chair and slammed it into the side of her bare body. Two of the legs broke off and he continued to hit her until the chair completely fell apart in his hand. Ava lay in the corner, her knees pulled up to her chest in the fetal position, blood trickling down her hip and stomach, but she didn't shed a tear.

"I've paid, Two Peace," she said softly. "Haven't I paid?"

"Yeah, you paid," said Two Peace sounding disgusted. He picked up the syringe, rubber strap and vile off the table and threw it at Ava in the corner. He buckled his pants and grabbed his backpack off the table before heading toward the door. He looked down at Ava on all fours clamoring to collect the supplies she earned. He reared his leg back and kicked Ava in the stomach. She fell into the corner holding her gut and gasped for breath.

"Fuckin' junkie whore," said Two Peace. He slammed the door behind him and was gone.

After a few minutes Ava caught her breath and strained to push herself off the floor to sit up. She gently touched her face to make sure she was still in one piece. She held her hands out like taking communion and the blood from her mouth pooled in her palms. Disregarding her injuries she got on with her quest. Ava picked up the rubber tubing, wrapped it around her left arm and cinched it tight with her teeth. She drew the liquid from the vile, thumped it several times with her middle finger, then plunged the needle into a pulsing vein. Ava lay back on the ground, outstretched, and let the warmth race through her naked, bruised and bloodied body. She slowly closed her eyes and accepted her fate.

Chapter Thirty-Four

After a sleepless night cruising the worst areas in town, Able stormed through the front door to the Charleston Police Station on Lockwood Boulevard and hurried to the duty desk. He slammed a stack of flyers on the desk and demanded they circulate them to the next shift. Sergeant Kerny, a stout, red faced Irishman, who followed his father and grandfather into law enforcement, was not in the mood for brash civilian behavior.

"Who do you think you're talking to, buddy?" he said in an unforgiving tone. "What makes your problem more important than theirs?" He pointed to a waiting area and holding cell, which were both filled to capacity.

"I'm sorry, officer," Able said. "But this woman has been missing since yesterday after she left her treatment center in Summerville. They think she came back to Charleston to find a fix. Her parents are worried sick. If they don't find her soon it may be too late. I've been driving around Charleston all night and haven't seen any sign of her."

Sergeant Kerny saw the desperation in his eyes. His son went through a similar ordeal years ago and was only saved by the grace of God. He scanned the flyer quickly, then called for another officer to distribute them to the next shift and to those in the holding cell on drug charges.

"We'll find her," he said very matter of factly. "There's only a few places in town where you can get what she's looking for. I'll radio cars in the area to keep a look out and to pick up their usual suspects."

"Thank you, Sergeant, thank you," Able said shaking his hand. "What can I do to help?"

"You can wait to hear from me," he said. "That's it, you sit and wait."

Of course, Able agreed and thanked the Sergeant again, then got in his car and headed to the rough side of town again to continue to scan the streets.

Old Charleston wasn't that big, but it could be confusing with all the one way streets and dead ends. He drove slowly up and down the dark streets. Many of the streetlights had been taken out by well-thrown rocks or the steady hand of a shooter. The sales in that neighborhood were best transacted in the shadows and many cursed the moonlit nights for casting too much light on their activities.

A group of six young black men stood on the corner smoking cigarettes and laughing. As Able drove by they all stopped and stared. He briefly thought about asking if they had seen Ava, but thought it best to keep moving. They watched him for a half block before resuming their social gathering.

His cell phone rang and he fumbled to answer it.

"Mr. Curran," said an official sounding voice. "Sergeant Kerny here, sir. We found a blonde female fitting your friend's description. She's in rough shape, sir, but I wanted you to know she's been found on Nassau Street."

"I'm only a few blocks from Nassau Street, Sergeant," Able said anxiously. "I'm on my way."

The screech of tires flowed through the phone as Able made a quick U-turn. Sweat beaded on his forehead and his pulse quickened as his mind raced. He turned left on Alexander and sped towards Nassau Street and prayed that Ava was still alive.

"Be careful, Mr. Curran," barked the Sergeant. "We don't need you getting hurt too."

By the time he arrived, maybe one minute since the phone call, there were two police cars, an investigation unit and an ambulance already parked and idling in front of an abandoned row house.

A woman with Charleston CSI emblazoned across the back of her jacket bent down in the middle of the street and shined a small light on a shimmering glob of liquid.

She opened her crime scene case, took out a cotton swab and vile, then took a sample. The glob was the color of molasses and had a pungent smell. It was still fresh, maybe just a few hours old. She crouched over the glob and looked in all directions before training her light on an object twenty feet away. She used her tweezers to pick up a crumpled and empty bag of Red Man chewing tobacco. She placed it in an evidence bag and marked it as item #2.

The female investigator walked over to the commanding officer with her two pieces of evidence.

"Captain, this will probably sound politically incorrect," she said a bit hesitant. "But, I don't think many gang members around here are chewing Red Man these days. Do you? I've got an empty pouch and saliva."

"That fits," said the Captain. "Ray Ray here said a white guy in an old pickup truck dropped off a blonde last night. Said he couldn't get out of this neighborhood fast enough. Ok, let's run a test on the saliva and see if our boy has a record. Take him with you."

The Captain pushed Ray Ray against his squad car, quickly cuffed him and pushed him in the back of the CSI vehicle.

"Hey, man!" shouted Ray Ray. "I go helping y'all out and you treat me like shit. What's up with you, cop? Why the fuck you taking me in? I done told you all I know about that blonde bitch, man."

Able attempted to get out of his car to see what was going on. He pushed the door open with one hand and still had his phone in the other. Before the door cracked open more than a few inches a police officer stormed over to stop him.

"Stay in your vehicle, sir! Stay in your vehicle!" he yelled. "This is an active crime scene." The officer pushed the door back closed as Able looked up through the window in frustration.

"Mr. Curran!" yelled Sergeant Kerny still on the line. "Mr. Curran, sir! Do you read me, sir. Are you there?"

"Yes, yes, Sergeant," stammered Able. "Yes, I'm here. I hear you."

An EMS technician quickly ran from the abandoned row house and swung open the back doors of the ambulance. He jumped inside and went through his checklist to ready for the new patient. A moment later two other EMS workers carried a gurney out the front door and down the few steps to the broken and cracked sidewalk. Stark white sheets were draped over Ava's body and large splatters of blood stood out in contrast. Two wide black straps were cinched tightly across her legs and torso. Her blonde hair was matted and streaked in red. She did not move.

"It's best you go home now and wait to hear from the family. Sir? Mr. Curran, sir?"

The ambulance doors slammed shut. The siren blasted loudly and echoed through the canyon of poverty . . . a familiar sound to the locals. It raced eastward toward Charleston General just a few miles away. The small crowd scattered. The show was over.

Able clicked his phone off without saying goodbye. He lay it on the dash of his car and bowed his head against the steering wheel. His eyes filled with tears and he began to weep. He hugged the steering wheel and prayed to God for her to be okay.

"Please, God," he pleaded. "Please don't take her away . . . not like this . . . please, God."

Chapter Thirty-Five

The stranger glanced up at the cracked rearview mirror of the old truck to find a patrol car on his tail. Instinctively, his heart began to race and beads of sweat formed on his brow. He briefly thought of trying to outrun the cop, but thought better of it. He'd been in trouble with law before and didn't want to make things worse. The last conviction of disorderly conduct got him three months in jail after the judge invoked the "three strikes" rule. He had sworn to fly right ever since.

Blue lights flashed brightly. He pulled the old pickup over on the shoulder, turned off the ignition and put both hands out the driver side window to show that he was unarmed. He knew the procedure.

"Do not move," the young officer shouted as he approached slowly, gun drawn. "Keep your hands where I can see 'em."

The officer walked slowly, training his weapon on the driver, then the passenger side, then back to the driver. After the all clear, the officer directed the man out of the truck and on the ground. Arms and legs out-stretched. He patted him down for weapons, but only found a tattered wallet, a half empty box of Marlboro Lights and an Uncle Buck pocket knife. The officer aimed his flashlight into the truck and scanned the floorboard and seats. He looked past the worn work jacket, the multiple fast food bags, the old thermos on the torn bucket seat and concentrated on a brown leather pocket book with a gold clasp lying on the floorboard. The officer walked around to the passenger side to collect the purse. He dumped the contents on the hood of the truck and riffled through a morass of lipsticks, a compact, mascara, sunglasses and other odds and ends. He unsnapped the alligator wallet and leafed through a variety of department store credit cards, three Visa cards, two American Express cards and a South Carolina driver's license that read Ava Gardner Dubose.

"Sir, please put your hands behind your back," said the officer rather politely. "You're coming downtown for questioning."

"I didn't do nothing," said the truck driver. "I just give her a lift, that's all, I didn't do nothing. She left that purse when I dropped her off."

The stench of the holding cell meandered through the hallway and was unavoidable to passers-by. Drunks, petty thieves, murderers and rapists were all held in three rooms down a stale, dank hallway. The police separated the intoxicated college kids from the thieves and the thieves from the murderers and rapists, but they all barked at each other like junkyard dogs through the open bars.

The truck driver was put in the middle cell and he sat quietly in the corner. He wanted to avoid all eye contact, follow directions and get home as soon as possible. Willie Barnhill had lived a hard life and spent plenty of time in jail over the years. He was only fifty, but easily could pass for sixty-five with his graying hair, deep cut wrinkles from smoking and several teeth missing. He lived in a single wide trailer in North Charleston and scraped by on his paltry earnings as a mechanic for a small gas station. He had never been married and rarely had any female companionship that didn't cost him $50 a throw. He thought it was his lucky day when Ava Dubose fell into his lap, but it became one of the worst days of his already hard life.

"Willie Barnhill," barked an officer at the cell door. "Get up here. Now!"

Willie slowly rose from the hard, uncomfortable bench and shuffled his way to the front of the holding cell. He looked at the officer, but did not say a word.

"Let's go," said the officer as he opened the steel door and closed it quickly with a loud clang. "Interrogation room three," he said pointing down the hallway with a billy club in his hand. "Move it."

Willie entered the room and sat down at the small table. He fidgeted in his chair for a moment as the officer stood silently at the door.

"Could I get a glass of water?" Willie asked nervously.

Without speaking the officer went to the corner water cooler and filled a small paper cup with cold, clear water. He offered it to Willie who drank it in one gulp, wiped his mouth with his sleeve and nodded to the officer in appreciation.

"How about a cigarette?" asked Willie.

"No smoking in here," barked the officer. "Now shut up!"

Another thirty minutes passed in silence until a detective threw open the door and stormed in. The officer left the room and the detective walked in a slow circle around Willie and the table. Willie stared straight ahead looking at the stark white wall. Finally, he looked up at the detective.

"I didn't do nothing to that girl," he said in a weak voice.

"Shut the fuck up, asshole!" screamed the detective. "You don't talk unless I tell you to talk! Do you hear me? I said do you hear me, asshole?"

"Yes sir, yes sir," said Willie softly.

The detective paced around the room for another few minutes then stopped and stood directly behind Willie. He leaned down and spoke in hushed tones into his ear.

"You're a bad drunk, Willie. Your record shows several drunk and disorderly, a few speeding tickets and a larceny charge when you were twenty," he said matter-of-factly. "So, tell me Willie, what in the fuck were you doing with a Charleston socialite yesterday and why did we find her near death on Nassau Street three hours ago?"

"I didn't hurt that girl. She wouldn't even let me touch her." Willie pleaded as his blood pressure spiked. "I didn't do nothing. Promise. I just give her a lift, that's all. I just give her a lift."

"If you didn't do anything, Willie," the detective barked in his ear. "Then why did we find her naked and beaten senseless with a needle of bad heroin in her arm. That doesn't sound like nothing to me!"

Willie pleaded with the detective to believe him. He told his story of picking up the classy looking lady who was hitch hiking and dropping her off on Nassau Street like she wanted. He told the detective that he told her not get out in that neighborhood, but she needed her fix. She needed it so bad that she jumped out of his truck and left her pocketbook behind.

The detective knew he was questioning the wrong man. He knew Willie was a bad drunk from time to time and ended up in jail to sleep it off, but that was about it. The detective had Willie stay in lockup overnight, then released him the next day when his story was confirmed by other witnesses who saw him drop off Ava and speed away.

Willie picked up his valuables as he left the station . . . his wallet, keys to the truck and a half pack of Marlboro cigarettes. The cops would not release his pocket knife. The moment he stepped outside he banged a cigarette out of the carton and lit it quickly. He inhaled deeply and enjoyed his first smoke in 24-hours. He got into his old, broken down pickup truck and drove straight to his favorite watering hole. The boys at the bar were about to get an earful.

Chapter Thirty-Six

Palmetto Memorial Gardens
Charleston, South Carolina

—February 1994—

Able waited until everyone had paid their respects to the family and the last limousine pulled away. He approached the casket slowly as if it may suddenly spring open and everyone would jump out of hiding to laugh at him. Ava would lead in the "gotcha." He gently folded himself into a chair directly in front of the casket and cradled his head in his hands. He sat there for several minutes as the realization that she was actually gone set in. The rain fell harder now and the steady drone of rain drops pelting the green canvas tent filled his head. Able reached out and laid an ungloved hand on the glossy mahogany casket. It was cold and damp. He stroked the casket like it was her mane of long luxurious hair. He did not cry, but the weight of his sadness knocked him to one knee. He pressed his head against the casket and kneeled at the altar of Ava, hand out-stretched over the crown of the casket as if giving her one last embrace. Able held on as his head raced with thoughts of love, guilt, anger.

"Goddammit," he said in a soft voice. "Goddammit!" he shouted skyward as he crumbled to his knees.

A moment later Able felt a hand on his shoulder and quickly turned at being startled. He looked up with a frightened and uneasy look on his face.

"It's me, darling," said Able's wife, June. "It's nearly dinner time, darling. You've been gone since noon and I was worried about you."

"What? Dinner time? Everyone just left," said Able sounding confused.

"The funeral ended four hours ago, darling. The reception at the Dubose house is over, too. I stopped by there with a casserole for their dinner and they said you weren't at the service. When you weren't back at the house I asked my mother to watch Maggie and I went out looking for you."

Able slowly stood up and faced his loving wife. She reached out and held his face in her soft, caring hands. June knew better than anyone what he was going through.

She was accepting of his obsession from the beginning, because having most of Able was better than none at all. That's how she justified it anyway. They looked at each other deeply and their eyes welled with tears. They grabbed each other and hugged tightly. She ran her hand through his rain soaked hair and kissed his wet cheek.

"You know I will always be here for you, darling, always," she whispered in his ear. "You are the love of my life. You are MY life."

Able buried his head in the nape of his wife's neck and cried for the second time that day. She held on tightly and stroked his hair while the man she loved cried silently in her arms. His shoulders steadily shook. She held him even tighter. He did not cry for the loss of Ava, but for the tremendous love that he felt for his wife and daughter. During all the years he spent trying to save Ava he didn't realize that he needed saving, too. June saved him from himself and the birth of Maggie gave him purpose. The void Ava left in his heart that day was quickly filled with the undying love his family poured into him. He had always loved his family, but Ava kept a little piece of him for herself. She would never let him go as long as she drew breath . . . as long as he was held by her spell. Able did not fully realize it until this very moment.

"I'm sorry, June."

“Sorry for what, darling?”

“I’m sorry for not giving you all of me. You and Maggie deserve all of me and I’ve held back. No matter how little, I’ve held back. Can you ever forgive me?”

“Able Curran, you have been everything to Maggie and me. You’re a wonderful husband and an amazing father. Look at me, Able,” she said grabbing his shoulders and leaning over to catch his downcast eyes. “Your only mistake was falling in love with the wrong woman fifteen years ago. That’s all, darling. Do not apologize for being a loving and trusting man. That is why I love you so much.”

Able cocked his eyes upward and saw the sweet smile of his beautiful wife. He pivoted his head back upright and gazed into her deep green eyes. His mouth curled up in a shy smile and his eyes glistened with admiration and affection.

“I don’t know another woman who would put up with my bullshit.”

“Well, compared to some of our friends, this is a walk through the tulips,” June laughed to lighten the mood. “If you only knew what went on all over Charleston it would blow your ever-loving mind. A few hours at girl’s night out is like watching an entire season of *The Young and the Restless*. I’ll take you and your bullshit any day of the week.”

June wrapped her arms around Able and they sunk into each other with a long, loving hug. They pressed their lips together and kissed like they were at the altar again . . . simple, sweet and heartfelt. Able took her hand and led her back across the cemetery as tombstones stood sentry along the way. They stopped at June's car and kissed again like high school kids at the end of a first date. They were giddy with excitement before realizing again their surroundings.

"Let's pick up Maggie and head to the cottage for a few days," said Able with a smile. "You know how being at the cottage always brings us back to earth."

"That sounds wonderful. I love the beach in the wintertime. I can make a big family breakfast in the morning, while you build a cozy fire."

Their cottage at Folly Beach was a classic low country house at the southeast point of the island. It was on the ocean, but had views of the river and sound, too. It was a panoramic view of God's handiwork with sand, sea and marsh. They would sip coffee on the front porch and watch the sun come up in the morning. Their days ended with a bottle of wine on the back porch as the marsh glows pink and orange with the setting sun. It was the perfect place to forget all that life threw at them and to just enjoy the beauty of creation. Able loved the cottage if for no other reason than that it reconnected him to his family. Folly time was family time and nothing else seemed to matter.

Able, June and Maggie walked down the boardwalk to the beach in front of the cottage. Jelly Roll, their chocolate lab, ran headlong into a crashing wave. The frigid water had no affect and he bounded through the surf chasing sandpipers along the shore.

It was 7:00 a.m. and the sun dripped like orange sherbet across the horizon. It was a cloudless morning and the early blue-gray sky hinted to a beautiful day ahead. Able picked up a baseball bat sized piece of driftwood and heaved it into the ocean. Jelly Roll was up for the challenge and leaped over an oncoming wave before splash down. He caught the piece of wood and dragged it back to shore. Jelly Roll dropped the drift wood at his master's feet. Able stopped dead in his tracks. He looked up and saw June and Maggie walking hand in hand along the sand fifty yards ahead. June draped the excess of her cardigan sweater around Maggie's shoulders and they walked huddled together in the crisp morning air. He smiled wide as he heard their laughter in the distance. He took it all in . . . the beauty of the morning, the simple excitement of his dog, the love he felt for his wife and daughter. This was the life he always wanted. It was there the whole time, but he was blinded by temptation . . . by fate ball.

"Come on, Daddy!" yelled Maggie from down the beach. "Catch up, catch up!"

"I'm coming, honey bun!"

Able broke into a half-jog as June and Maggie stopped to wait. They waved their arms at him like a coach at a track meet to go faster. He sprinted the last thirty yards and was greeted by smiles and laughter. He bent over and rested his hands on his knees to catch his breath. The cold morning air burned as it rushed into his lungs.

"I've got you, Daddy," Maggie said trying to prop him up. "You'll be okay."

"I've got you too, darling," said June as she wrapped her arm around Able and smiled.

Able smiled and stood upright. He took them each by the hand and swung his arms playfully as they walked. Maggie giggled for no particular reason and they all laughed at her youthful giddiness.

It was going to be a beautiful day, thought Able. *It was going to be a beautiful life.*

About the Author

Adam W. Jones was born in Raleigh, NC and is one of five siblings who all were brought up to be free thinkers. After a year-long sojourn across Europe after high school, he attended the University of North Carolina at Chapel Hill. He finally finished with a degree in Journalism and Mass Communications after some starts and stops in his college career. He worked for fifteen years in advertising and marketing before starting his own real estate firm in 2002. Adam has had children's and travel stories published in a variety of local and regional magazines throughout the years, but this is his first novel. Early versions of *Fate Ball* sat on the shelf collecting dust for years until recently, when he became determined to finish it.

Adam is a husband and a father of two young girls. He lives in Chapel Hill, NC with his family and their two dogs.